PARANORMAL COZY MYSTERY

Wheels & Dirty Deals

TRIXIE SILVERTALE

Sittin' On A Goldmine
Productions L.L.C.

Sittin' On A Goldmine Productions, L.L.C.

pr@sittinonagoldmine.co

www.sittinonagoldmine.co

This is a work of fiction. Names, characters, places, and incidents are products of the author's imagination or are used fictitiously and are not to be construed as real. Any resemblance to actual events, locales, business establishments, organizations, or persons, living or dead, is entirely coincidental.

ISBN: 978-1-952739-66-8

Cover Design © Sittin' On A Goldmine Productions, L.L.C.

Cover design by Melony Paradise of Paradise Cover Design

Trixie Silvertale
Wheels and Dirty Deals: Paranormal Cozy Mystery : a novel / by Trixie Silvertale — 1st ed.
[1. Paranormal Cozy Mystery — Fiction. 2. Cozy Mystery —

Fiction. 3. Amateur Sleuths — Fiction. 4. Private Investigator — Fiction. 5. Wit and Humor — Fiction.] 1. Title.

My hands shake with disbelief. My heart races like a freight train. Steadying my finger to press the speed dial for *Secret Alchemist* seems a monumental task. I hit speaker and collapse against my pillow.

My mentor answers on the first ring. I plow ahead. "Silas, I had an absolute bonkers dream. I need to know what it means."

"Good afternoon, Mizithra. I trust you are well?" His ability to avoid answering the question and somehow simultaneously teach me a lesson is not lost on me.

"I don't have time for manners. It was a dream about my mother. And a powerful magical — maybe alchemical — object."

Suddenly, I have his full attention. "Are you

quite certain this was merely a dream? It may have been a communication with your mother's spirit. Has Coraline Moon previously spoken to you in this manner?"

It's not often I find myself at a loss for words. His suggestion that this strange vision could be more than the wishful thinking of a girl orphaned at eleven nearly stops my heart. "Not like this. This time, I felt her in her physical form. She hugged me. Then she gave me the strangest message."

Silas harrumphs, and a ragged exhale followed by pensive silence swallows up nearly a minute before he replies.

"We acquire additional knowledge about your abilities with each passing day. What you have described could be astral travel. An out-of-body experience. In my understanding of the arcane and the spirit world, I believe this to have been a visitation. Not merely a phantasm of dreamland. Do you recall the message?"

"I will never forget it as long as I live." The hairs on the back of my neck bristle with anticipation.

My mentor's tone remains calm but stern. "You must repeat it word for word. Each syllable spoken by the energies on the other side of the veil carries an import our minds can scarcely comprehend."

Sinking into the precious memory of my mother's touch is easy. I never want to leave this place.

As her arms loosen and her hands slide downward, she grips my fingers in hers. Gentle, dark eyes seem to stare through mine — to my soul. Her beautiful British voice fills my head.

"My sweet girl, I have learned of a powerful relic. On this side of the veil, it is known as the Oracle of Return. Find it. Speak my name into its ear. I shall return to you. Whole. Unblemished. As though I never left."

"Silas, could it be . . .?"

CHAPTER 1

"GRAMS! Just because you traveled all over Europe with Max, your second of five husbands, doesn't mean taking Erick to Europe is going to end in our divorce!"

"It wasn't divorce that ended Max and me." The ghost of my not-as-dearly-departed-as-everyone-thinks grandmother drifts toward the ceiling of the plush apartment, which lies hidden away behind the secret bookcase leading to the bookshop I inherited.

"I'm sorry for your loss, Grams." An ache strangles my breath. I don't even want to imagine losing Erick . . . No. Nope.

Myrtle Isadora gazes down, her translucent eyes swirling with love and sorrow in equal measure. "Max was undeniably himself. To the bitter end." She sniffs sharply. "Who knows? If I hadn't lost my kidney in our tragic car accident, I might never have gotten sober. Without my sobriety, I never would've had a chance to have a son. Without Jacob . . ." Her ethereal voice drifts off.

You don't have to be a psychic to pick up the unspoken thought. If my father had never been born, I would never have been born. I'm not vain enough to think that the world couldn't survive without Mitzy Moon, but I know how full and wonderful my life has been since discovering an unexpected family in almost-Canada.

"I wish you could've met my mother." My gaze follows an osprey as it flies past the window and reels out over the great lake tucked into the harbor behind Bell, Book & Candle Bookshop. "Coraline Moon was everything I wanted to be when I grew up."

Grams swooshes down from her high perch and wraps her glowing limbs around me in a hum of loving energy. "Nonsense! You're exactly who you're meant to be. Wonderful. Amazing. The very best granddaughter any grandmother could ever wish for." Ghost tears well in the corners of her eyes like storm surge against a dam, and I hop out of the rolly chair in front of the computer as I slide from her ghostly embrace.

"No tears. You know I missed the chance to slip

you an afterlife handkerchief." We share a wistful grin as we both recall the moment she almost faded away, and it took the concerted effort of all those in the inner "ghost" circle to hold her on this side of the veil.

A mournful sigh escapes my lips. "My mother was amazing, though."

"I have no doubt." Ghost-ma claps her hands as though I've given the best Oscar acceptance speech of the night. "She raised you!"

"She barely had a chance to raise me. I was so little when I lost her. And then almost seven years in foster care! It's a wonder I didn't end up on the wrong side of the law."

As though the mere suggestion of law enforcement can summon him, the secret bookcase door slides open, and in saunters the tall drink of water that is my smart, sexy, somewhat dreamy husband, Erick Harper.

Grams squeals. "The vacation!" She flies toward the computer, too frantic to summon enough corporeal form to click the mouse.

Thankfully, Erick can't hear Isadora, and my fiendish feline is a step ahead.

Pyewacket leaps from the floor to the desktop in a single blur of tan, furry excellence. His powerful paw smashes the mouse as though it were a living creature, and, after completing his amazing act, the wise caracal flops down on the keyboard, obscuring most of the screen with his broad head and black-tufted ears.

Erick gazes from Pyewacket to me and chews the inside of his cheek, as his luscious blue eyes survey the situation with seasoned expertise. "If I was still sheriff of Birch County, I would definitely suspect a cybercrime underway."

Eager to change the subject, I rush toward him, tripping over my own foot and falling into his arms like one of those damsels in a bodice-ripper novel.

He chuckles, and his voice drops an octave. "You don't have to ask me twice, Mrs. Moon."

Despite my status as a married woman, my cheeks flush with heat. "Knock it off, Harper. I tripped, as per usual, and you happened to be the beneficiary. There was no salacious plot."

Of course, the minute I deny a salacious plot — Oh, the human mind is a powerful visualizer!

His arms slip tighter around my waist, and his soft, pouty lips curve into a mischievous grin as he leans in.

Ghost-ma's chuckle ruins the moment, and I wriggle away in a fluster of embarrassment. "As you might've guessed, we're not alone."

My husband can neither see nor hear the ghost of Myrtle Isadora. However, it doesn't stop him from glancing around the room. "Good afternoon,

Isadora. I don't suppose you'd be willing to write me a brief message on one of your special 3 x 5 cards and tell me what Mitzy was up to?"

If only he could see her. Her chosen ghost age of thirty-five, despite her physical death in her late sixties, combined with the giggle of a schoolgirl, makes her burgundy silk-and-tulle Marchesa burial gown look more like a Halloween costume than fashion history.

The small tear in the hem of her gown and the missing silver Valentino slingback interrupt my momentary amusement. It may have been almost two years ago, but it feels like yesterday when my séance gone wrong nearly ended with the loss of my grandmother's ghost. But that's another story.

"Looks like you have something on your mind, Harper."

He laughs lightly. "Never try to fool a psychic. That's what they tell me, anyway. I just came from Myrtle's Diner, and Odell said that they've added two roller derby teams from Pin Cherry Harbor to the Northwoods League."

Ghost-ma rips across the bookshop and straight through Erick, sending ghost chills down both of his arms.

"Grams! Take it easy."

"Oh dear! Tell him I'm sorry. I got so excited! You know I used to play, right?"

"Grams is sorry, and thrilled, and wants to remind us all she used to be a derby girl."

Erick nods. "Oh, Odell told me some stories. Apparently, Tipsy Kitty was the fastest jammer in the league."

Isadora hoots with laughter and pride.

My jaw hangs as slack as the waistband on a pair of pants in an "after" photo. "What the heck is a jammer?"

My patient husband nods with understanding. "I got a quick tutorial from Odell. Here's what I know. There are six skaters on the track for each team. Four of them are blockers. One is the pivot and one skater from each team wears a fabric cover with a star — called 'panties' — on their helmet. Those are the jammers."

"Whoa. Whoa." My non-athletic head is spinning. "Jammers? Panties? Blockers?"

"You know how it is, Moon. Every sport has its lingo. The point is the jammers have to get past the blockers and make as many laps around the track as they can in two minutes."

"The game only lasts two minutes? Sounds like the most foolish sport in history."

"No. No. That's just one jam. They play for ninety minutes with—"

A loud, bored exhale escapes my lips. "Give it

up, Harper. You've lost me already. If I can't see it in action, I can't follow."

An amused expression softens his firm jaw. "Good news. The local league team is skating an exhibition bout tonight in the gymnasium at the community college. Should I get tickets?"

Unable to erase the image of Cameron Diaz in *Charlie's Angels*, I instantly respond, "I love tickets."

CHAPTER 2

Cut to—

"Moon! Come on!" Erick's voice drifts up from the first floor of our three-story walk-up.

"I'm coming! Keep your shorts on, Harper."

"Is Isadora up there with you?" His voice is mostly a moan. "We're going to a derby bout, not the Met Gala."

A fit of giggles causes me to smear mascara across my left cheek. The Met Gala. That guy wouldn't know a Met Gala from a high-school prom. "You distracted me. Now I have to start my makeup all over!"

The sound of heavy footsteps on the staircase sends me into hyper-speed.

"Come on. We're gonna miss the opening

lineup announcement. Odell said that's the best part."

Swiping smeared mascara from my cheek, I shove the wand into the dispenser, twist, and bolt for the stairs. By the time I'm down the top flight, Erick is on the second-floor landing, hands on his hips like a stern mother in the 1950s.

"Simmer down, June Cleaver. I'm sure Odell only remembers opening lineup shenanigans because Grams put on a show for him. Let's not get into the weeds on that one."

Running past him, I reach the first floor and shout, "What's taking you so long, Harper? We'll miss the best part."

His thundering footfalls race up behind me as he scoops his arms tightly around my middle, and I fail to escape his clutches. Resting his chin on my shoulder, he whispers low and gravelly. "Don't tempt fate. I think your mouth is writing checks your body can't cash."

We both chuckle at the excellent *Top Gun* reference before he kisses my neck.

"We better get out of here, hubby."

He grabs my hand and leads me out to the 1968 copper-brown Chevy Nova SS warming up in the alley between my bookstore and my father's Restorative Justice Foundation.

It's a short drive to the Birch County Community College, and Erick fills every moment with additional tidbits about the rules of women's roller derby. He may as well be slinging an extra gallon of water over Niagara Falls. No one notices, or retains a single bit of information, least of all me.

When he turns into the car park, I'm shocked to see the normally half-empty parking lot overflowing with vehicles.

"Is there something else going on tonight? I mean, besides this roller game."

Erick gives his car a signature rev before turning it off and sniffs sharply as he pulls the key from the ignition. "No way. These are all fans. Everyone loves flat-track roller derby. I'm telling you, you'll get hooked."

Somehow I doubt it, but I eagerly take his offered hand and let him escort me into the gymnasium.

The bleachers are extended on either side of the basketball court to accommodate the maximum capacity crowd. On top of the highly polished wood floor sits a series of interlocking squares that have formed a temporary roller rink surface, and plastic flag rope runs along the sidelines, separating the stands from the track. Whoa. This is definitely more serious than I imagined.

My hubby beams like a kid filling up his second

pillowcase with Halloween candy as he tugs me to a seat on the bleachers.

Just in time . . .

"Ladies, gentlemen, panty chasers, and derby darlings, welcome to the Northwoods Roller Derby League!"

Thunderous applause echoes from both sides of the gymnasium. A large group on the opposite wall leaps to their feet and stomps out a kick-kick-clap rhythm until the announcer calls for quiet.

"Skating for the newest team in the league, the Pin Cherry Rink Rashers, your lead jammer, Bam Wow!"

A short, athletic girl skates in from the hallway. Orange and black hair flutters from under her helmet as she races around the track.

My side of the gymnasium goes crazy.

"Your lead blocker, Silence of the Jams!"

A girl about my size, healthy hips and all, powers onto the track. Her low center of gravity and aggressive expression cause me to lean back in my seat and gulp.

The rest of the Pin Cherry Rink Rashers perform similar moves as their names are called.

"And now, the Broken Rock Slammer Jammers!"

Crossing my arms and lifting one eyebrow, I exhale. Their name isn't quite as cool as our team.

Listen to me, "our team." Looks like hubby was right. I'm destined to be a roller derby fan.

As the announcer calls out the players, my jaw ratchets open and I struggle to swallow.

Finally, I blurt, "The opposing team has a couple of very large blockers. I wouldn't want to be skating against them!"

Erick snuggles close and whispers for my ears only, "Neither would I."

"Aaaaaaand, here's your head referee, One Man Wolf Pack, to get things started."

The referee skates onto the track, blows his whistle, and both teams line up their jammer on one line, pivot and blockers on another.

The whistle screams once. It's like watching that moment when popcorn just starts popping!

The pivots set the pace, blockers form a wall, and when the quick double whistle sounds, the two jammers surge forward with incredible strength and speed. Everything happens at once.

"Here comes your hometown girl Bam Wow, and she hip-checks Animal Kooky off the track to take lead jammer status!"

The crowd goes wild.

Broken Rock's jammer, Animal Kooky, bounces to her feet in a flash, circles back, and reenters the track.

"Looks like that move is going to cost her, folks.

Dukes up Daisy is lining up to send Bam Wow sprawling."

The spectators collectively hold their breath.

"Hold on to your programs, folks! It's a perfectly executed apex jump by Bam Wow!" Cheers echo through the gym. "Rink Rashers are taking care of business."

The announcer sounds like a home team fan.

"Bam Wow takes the lead and covers a lot of track. She's scoring points faster than a skeet baller at Chuck E. Cheese."

Suddenly, One Man Wolf Pack blasts two sharp and short notes.

The ladies skate to their respective benches.

Glancing at Erick, I throw my hands in the air. "That's it? What happened?"

He points to the scoreboard. "We scored twelve points. Our jammer called off the jam as soon as she made that last pass. That means the other team couldn't score any more points."

"Oh. You didn't ever tell me that part."

His shoulders sag as his hangdog head wags back and forth. "Maybe you weren't listening."

"Fair enough." Determined to avoid any additional scolding, I use my handy psychic replay to go over those ramblings on the drive to the gym. Whoa! He did cover a lot of ground. I'm up to speed now.

The next jam begins. Silence of the Jams has the star cover on her helmet. "Hey, why does she have the panties? I thought she was a blocker."

Erick twists his torso to get a better look at me. "So you were listening. Whoever has that star cover on their helmet at the beginning of the jam is the jammer. They switch it up, because jammers have to skate so fast. It's better for them if they can sit out a jam or two. Recharge their battery."

"Cool. I wonder if Grams has any videos of her games?"

Erick places his hand on my knee and gives a gentle squeeze. "It's called a *bout*, sweetie."

My skin tingles at his touch, and his words float uselessly past my eardrums.

At halftime, a bunch of little rug rats in adorable tiny skates come out to do a demonstration. Holding my breath, I'll admit I expect the worst.

The young girls skate flawlessly around the track. The announcer mentions they're not allowed to make contact like the women's league, but they still look pretty intimidating out there, zipping around the track and weaving between one another with the skill of Formula 1 drivers.

The tough tweens skate off, and the second half gets underway. My smile still holds admiration for the skill of those youngsters long after their exit.

Closing his hand over mine, Erick gazes at me with pure love. "Would you let our kids play a sport like this, Moon?"

Gulp. I've done a decent job of avoiding this conversation. As an orphan who didn't discover she had a family until her mid-twenties, I've never been all that pumped to venture into having children of my own. However, Erick has always hinted that kids were something he wanted. How am I gonna get out of this?

CHAPTER 3

I'm not sure if I make the next thing happen, or if serendipity simply loves me, but the guy behind us jumps up and spills popcorn and hot cocoa on Erick. The guy immediately sets down his refreshments and apologizes profusely.

When Erick turns around, the man gulps visibly. "Hey, Sheriff. I swear—"

"No worries, Billy. I'm not sheriff anymore, remember?"

"Oh yeah. Still . . . super sorry, dude. Super sorry. I just got super stoked, you know?"

All that "super" talk sends my mind wandering back to Sedona, Arizona, and my SUPERvisor Dean. I've never known anyone, before or since, that could get so super excited about coffee. The *good* old days. Spoiler alert: they weren't that good.

Life as a broke barista had about zero upside. I'm happy to pay it forward now that I'm a wealthy heiress with a philanthropic foundation. The universe gave me a great opportunity, and I'm not about to waste it.

Fingers wiggle in front of my face, and I know beyond a shadow of a doubt I've drifted off into one of my mind movies. "Sorry. What were you saying?"

Erick gives my shoulder a squeeze. "Gotta run down to the restroom and rinse off my shirt. If the bout ends, wait here. Okay?"

"Sure. Whatever."

The action on the track should be enough to pull anyone's gaze, but mine follows the backside of Erick Harper as he makes his way down the bleachers and out of the gym. My, oh my, that man can fill out a pair of jeans.

The derby bout draws to a close, and the Pin Cherry Rink Rashers reign supreme. Raucous cheers erupt, and the Rashers skate a victory lap on the track. Then everybody makes nice. Players from both teams shake hands, and people head toward the exits from the gymnasium.

As the crowd thins, I feel like the girl who didn't get asked to dance at homecoming. Hubby wanted me to wait here, but I feel like an idiot.

Stepping down bleachers, with the appropriate

amount of caution, I follow the remaining spectators back to the lobby. The home team has set up a couple of long folding tables, and the derby girls are signing calendars, T-shirts, and occasionally people!

Why not take a peek? I love good merch.

The crowd has thinned considerably, and there are only two stragglers at the far end of the second table. As I approach, the skaters are deep in conversation. The psychic hairs on the back of my neck instantly come to attention. They're definitely not speaking English. Which seems weird, because I thought they were local gals.

Casually sinking into one of my new-ish psychic abilities, I listen for the feel of the words rather than the actual words. In the past, this connection to meaning versus pronunciation has allowed me to understand languages I don't speak. There are many. I mean, I speak English and some Spanglish, which is a mix of Spanish and English, and . . . That's about it.

Rather than joy over their victory, the skaters' hushed tones are full of worry, anxiety, and a soupçon of fear.

They seem to be talking about someone named Attila the Hun.

Going out on a limb, I'm pretty sure they're not talking about the actual Attila the Hun.

"Excuse me."

Silence of the Jams and Celia Fate whip their heads toward me. A puppy covered in freshly dug up potting soil could not look this guilty.

"What language is that? It's very beautiful."

For a moment, their fear is palpable.

Silence of the Jams takes the question. "Hungarian. I learn it from my grandmother. We—"

"How cool." She's clearly lying through her teeth, and I want to put her mind at ease. "Anyway, how much for the T-shirts?"

In unison, they breathe a sigh of relief as Celia Fate points to the sign. "Twenty-five each, or two for fifty."

Does she realize that's not a deal? None of my business. Not the time to pinch pennies. "Sweet. I'll take two." Thumbing through the stacks to find my size, I grab one shirt that reads, "Hit like a girl. Play Derby," with a cute anime-style skater hip-checking a pin cherry tree and sending cherries flying through the air. The second shirt reads, "Give blood. Play derby."

Handing the money to Celia Fate, I smile and lean closer. "You guys are awesome. Seriously. I want to be you when I grow up."

Rather than the expected gratitude, my psychic senses take a gut punch of sadness when she reaches for the bills.

Weird. Maybe something's going on in her personal life.

Grabbing my T-shirts, I thank the team and hurry back to the gymnasium before Erick catches me. As I enter the brightly lit gym, a bellowing voice cuts through the din of the fans' departure. "Moon! Where's Harper?"

Glancing across the space, it's easy to see tall, confident Boomer, a deputy and sniper at the Broken Rock Sheriff's Station. He and Erick used to battle it out for the sharpshooter title. Since Erick retired, Boomer has been king of the target, and it's definitely gone to his pretty blond head.

Not wanting to appear rude, I hustle over and meet Boomer near the opposite exit doors. "Erick got some hot chocolate spilled on him and ran to the restroom to clean his shirt. He'll be back in a second."

"Good. He owes me a beer. Tell him to meet me at Final D."

Boomer waves, turns, and struts out.

This is all news to me. I had no idea we were going to Final Destination. I'm cool with it. For a dive bar, it's actually pretty great. I love playing a little pool after I've had a drink or two, and Lars, the owner, is an old friend.

My body seems to freeze in place, and I can almost hear the wheels spinning in my head. Wow!

I've lived in Pin Cherry long enough to have "old" friends. Yeesh. What's become of me?

If I didn't know Ghost-ma's spirit was tethered to the bookshop, I'd swear the voice in my head was a genuine ghost encounter. "You're settling down, sweetie. And you like it," says the crystal clear voice of Grams.

Erick bursts into the gymnasium. "Hey, I've got a favor to ask." He quickly closes the gap between us.

"Let me guess, you'd like to go to Final Destination. And you want to buy Boomer a beer?"

His grin fades and shock tilts his head. "Wow. Did you get an image in your mood ring? That's oddly specific, even for you."

The reference to the moody mood ring, which occupies the place where most gals wear their wedding band, warms my heart. The vintage 70s ring, with its mysterious smoky cabochon in the center of gold braided trim, was the very thing that triggered my odd psychic abilities. Once it took up residence on my left hand, it refused to be displaced.

The ring belonged to my grandmother, or so I'm told. One never knows if you're getting the whole truth and nothing but the truth when you hear stories from Myrtle Isadora Johnson Linder Duncan Willamet Rogers. Her colorful past is the stuff of legend.

I wish I could keep my features stern and confirm all the information came from a psychic hit, but I instantly break and spill my guts. "Boomer saw me waiting for you. He told me the whole deal. I'm happy to head over to Final D. It's been a while since I've had a chance to catch up with Lars."

Once again, Erick takes my hand and everything feels right with the world. We walk back to the Chevy Nova, and you didn't hear it from me, but he may have exceeded the speed limit on the way to our local haunt.

CHAPTER 4

THE SEEDY DIVE bar known as Final Destination is home to the blue-collar and outdoors-y crowd. And I say "known as" because the "s" is actually burned out on the neon sign. So it reads: "Final De_tination," which is probably far more accurate.

Despite all the red flags that scream, "run," there's a cozy, homey feel to the place — once you get past the aroma of stale peanuts and spilled beer.

The burly bartender, Lars, with salt-and-pepper Travis Tritt hair, stares at me for far longer than necessary before transforming from gruff barkeep to happy Labrador. "Could that be Daisy, my favorite waitress?"

His reference to a previous undercover gig I ran at his establishment does not go unnoticed by my husband. "Oh yeah, that's the one where you slugged me so hard I fell off the barstool, right?"

My cheeks transform with heat, and I look down at my high tops as I mumble, "I had to protect my cover, Johnny Law."

Erick and Lars enjoy a long guffaw at my expense.

Before we can unpack any more of that unpleasant memory, Boomer jogs across the bar and slaps Erick firmly on the back. "Well, if it isn't the former sheriff of Birch County!" He leans on the bar and sniffs sharply. "Give me a pint of your best. This guy's buying." He points his thumb in Erick's direction.

Lars is no spring chicken. He holds his ground and looks at my husband for approval.

Erick thumps Boomer on the back with equal, if not slightly more, force. "Give him whatever he wants, Lars. Successful private investigators have to take care of local law enforcement whenever they can."

I can't help but snicker with pride. It was a sick burn. And it doesn't look like Boomer has got anything in the tank for a comeback.

May as well pile on. "What are you doing hanging out in Pin Cherry, Boomer?"

He gratefully accepts a frosty mug of beer from Lars and turns to answer me. "My gal plays for the

Slammer Jammers. Harper and I have a standing bet. Winner buys."

Placing one hand on my ample hip, I tilt my head. "So what's the incentive to win? Are you telling me you got a whole derby team to take a fall so you could get a free beer?"

Without turning my head, all of my extra senses pick up on the sheer satisfaction emanating from my husband. Boomer, on the other hand, looks like he just got sucker punched.

Before he can recover, I make an announcement. "Keeping the standard bet in mind, I'm gonna rack 'em over there on table two. Winner buys me a sloe gin fizz. Who's brave enough to meet me on the felt?"

Boomer exchanges an overt eyebrow raise with Erick and shrugs. "All right, little lady. You got your work cut out for you. I've been playing pool since I was tall enough to see over the edge of the bumpers."

With a simple nod of my head, I walk over to the table where the ingenious use of some cut two-by-fours levels the open table and its green felt has more than a few thin spots. A low-hanging light above the worn billiard arena displays a popular beer logo and casts a dim illumination on the motley crew assembled on the surrounding stools, pushed against the wood-paneled walls.

After I rack the balls, I ask Boomer if he'd like to break.

"Nah, you go ahead. You need every advantage you can get."

This guy never met my foster brother, Jarrell. King of the grift. I've hustled more pool in my short life than Minnesota Fats. No need to tell Boomer. "Sure, thanks."

Heading over to the table, I fumble with the stick, drop the chalk, and almost scratch as I take a wild swipe at the cue ball. One lone striped ball falls into a corner pocket — almost as an afterthought.

He snorts. "Twenty bucks says I'm sinking the eight ball into the side pocket before you know what hit you."

Erick's face shows deep concern for his buddy, but he's behind Boomer and too far away to offer his friend any help.

"You sound pretty confident, Deputy. Make it fifty and I'll take that bet."

Boomer slaps his cash on the table, and I do the same. Pin Cherry Harbor is the town that tech forgot. Everybody carries cash in this town. You'd be hard-pressed to find a business that takes plastic. Things like old-fashioned paper passbooks at the bank and a majority of businesses that take *cash only* are par for the course around here.

He picks off the solids one by one, and a spasm of fear passes through me. Boomer is actually pretty good. I'm gonna have to forgo any additional ditzy snow-white blonde maneuvers and play for keeps.

Finally, Boomer scratches attempting to sink the seven ball.

Time for the razzle-dazzle.

I sink three stripes in rapid succession. Boomer is visibly shaken.

Taking a fresh position at the table, I set up for a shot that he can't quite visualize.

"Hey, I don't wanna help the competition, but you're making a big mistake."

I paint my features into a portrait of innocence, slide the pool cue behind my back, and arch over the table.

With one quick, confident stroke, I sink two balls in opposite corner pockets at once.

The color drains from Boomer's face.

Erick is all smiles now.

After a couple more minutes of unbridled embarrassment for my opponent, I clear the table of all stripes, call my pocket for the eight ball, and scoop the cash off the bumper. "Best two outta three?"

Boomer waves both hands in the air as though he's under arrest. "No way. I know a hustler when I see one. You can keep that money, but I'm not getting the wool pulled over my eyes twice."

From the corner of my eye, I notice Lars wheeling a machine out from behind the bar. Oh no! The karaoke machine.

Boomer and Erick clock the machine a mere three seconds after me.

Their eyes meet, and I know what's going to happen. Not like, "I have a bad feeling about this." Nope. This is every psychic fiber of my being knowing with absolute certainty.

I grab my sloe gin fizz and attempt to hide in the plethora of shadows.

Erick calls out, "Boomer, I think she's lost that loving feeling."

Oh no! It's happening.

They exchange additional banter, and it comes to my attention that Erick Harper is far more well-versed in film and television lore than I had originally suspected. Maybe being married to me is rubbing off on him, or maybe he was a secret cinephile long before he met this film-school dropout.

Lars flips on the machine, Erick and Boomer grab microphones, and the next thing I know, the serenade begins!

The night of our engagement is when I first discovered my husband had a knack for crooning. Later, he proved worthy of the stage in one of our undercover operations, and now he's using his hidden talent to embarrass the living daylights out of me. Grams will be thrilled.

The final bars of the song find Erick on his knees in front of me and my face to a shade of fuchsia I didn't even know existed.

Boomer takes a step back, humming along in harmony.

Erick brings the song to a close and plants a huge kiss on my shocked mouth.

Surprisingly, the smattering of anglers, dock-workers, and random city employees give my guy a standing ovation.

Erick takes a bow, and I play along, pretending to faint. Overcome by his display of affection. He scoops me into his arms, and the applause crescendos.

Laughter bounces off the low ceiling, and Lars claps loudest of all.

Who would've thought? Little orphan Mitzy. Finding her family in a town that feels more like home than any place has since her mother's arms. I'll never be able to repay my grandmother for her bravery and kindness in insisting that her lawyer, now my lawyer, Silas Willoughby, track me down after her passing to make sure that I found Pin Cherry Harbor.

Not only did I find the town, I found a whole wonderful life that I never imagined.

CHAPTER 5

SNEAKING IN AFTER our late night at Final D, I'm shocked there's no ghost banging at the door that separates our living quarters from the bookshop.

When we remodeled the old three-story printing museum into our first home together, I asked my mentor, Silas Willoughby, to place wards and sigils throughout the new construction to keep the ghost of Myrtle Isadora firmly on the outside.

It's not that I have any issue with her per se. But newlyweds need a bit of privacy, and I wanted to know that she could only enter our new home at my invitation.

Erick quickly stokes up a roaring fire in our third-floor primary suite while I slip into some cozy pajamas. I'd love to say they are my reindeer onesie pajamas — which are my coziest and most favorite — but I saw the sparkle in my husband's eye, and I'm pretty sure he's not planning on falling directly asleep.

The crackle of warmth spreads through the house, and the fragrance of burning cedar makes me smile as I slip into my version of something more comfortable.

As I saunter out of the bathroom in one of my new roller derby T-shirts, and not much else, his low chuckle shifts to a wicked smirk. "*Hit like a girl?* That's perfection, Moon. Get over here and let me inspect that T-shirt a little more closely."

My tummy tingles as I move into his embrace and inhale his citrus-woodsy scent. He nuzzles my neck, but my brain takes a sharp left. "Ooh! How about breakfast at Myrtle's Diner?"

His forehead rests heavy on my shoulder. "Moon! I'm giving you my best stuff over here, and you're thinking about breakfast?"

"Don't act surprised, Harper. Breakfast is the most important meal of the day."

Scooping me from the floor in one effortless motion, he mumbles something about me being the most important meal as he tosses me on the bed. Uh oh!

· · ·

WAKING AS THE LITTLE SPOON, with a growling tummy, brings a yawn and a huge stretch.

Erick tries to pull me back under the covers, but my appetite has spoken. "Time to feed the beast, Harper."

He rolls out of bed like a firefighter responding to a three-alarm fire! "Race ya!"

Barely avoiding a trip up with the blankets, I crawl out of bed and rush to the bathroom. "No fair! You had a head start."

"No excuses, Moon. Loser buys breakfast."

"What? Why does Boomer get the winner's bet and I get shafted?"

"Hey, if I play my cards right with you two, win or lose, I'll never pay for anything."

"Rude." My mouth may be complaining, but my body is kicking into overdrive. I'm dressed AND I have my shoes on when I run out of the bathroom.

"Winner!"

My triumphant husband looks up from his calm seat at the foot of the bed. "Oh, honey. You made a great effort. Did you look in the mirror?"

His clothes are clean, his boots are tied, and his long swath of blond bangs have been perfectly swooped into place with pomade.

I stumble back into the bathroom and glance at my reflection.

Laughter, so intense I snort, consumes me.

"I surrender."

"Understood."

After washing the smeared mascara from my cheeks and dragging a brush through my haystack of bone-white hair, I'm satisfied with my pre-sentable-ness.

"Ready."

He's off the bed and at my side in two steps. With a swift peck on the cheek, he turns and leads the way downstairs.

Our forward progress is barred by a stern-looking caracal. The black-tufts at the tips of his ears twitch, and his short tail whips left to right. Oddly, he makes no vocalization.

"What's the matter? Cat got your ton—?" I re-alize my mistake a moment too late.

The tan terror squeezes his eyelids to slits.

I shout, "Noooooooo," but his powerful jaw clamps down on whatever is in his mouth. What I hope is red food coloring sprays across the floor.

"Pyewacket! What has gotten into you?" As I plant my fists on my hips and have a standoff with the demon spawn, Pye drops the bottle on the ground and licks the color from his fur.

I'm boiling with rage, but also curious.

Erick slips past me and collects two rags, a bucket of soapy water, and some paper towels.

While he quietly cleans the mess, I attempt to get an explanation.

"Son, you better explain yourself."

Pye lifts up on his powerful hind legs and digs his claws into my derby tee.

"So, you're not a fan of derby? That's no reason to be a vandal."

"Ree-ow." Soft but condescending.

"All right. Clearly, I'm way off base." Tapping two fingers on my lips, I hope for psychic lightning to strike. "Hey! Is this about a case we don't have yet?"

"RE-OW!" Game on!

My shoulders sag as I exhale. "Next time, just drop the bottle. There's no need to act out."

Erick mops at a streak of red on my jeans. "Ah, it's only food coloring. It'll come out. Go easy on the big guy. He's only trying to help."

Mr. Cuddlekins nuzzles Erick. "Ree-oow." Conspiratorial agreement.

"I'm not a fan of you two teaming up! We'll add the mystery food coloring to the murder board — after we get a case. Deal?"

Pye continues to favor Erick with affection. "Reow." Can confirm.

My wonderful husband puts the bucket and rags in the sink, wipes his hands, and actually smiles.

"Let's walk, eh? It's pretty nice out."

"Pretty nice" is a true locals-only expression. I've learned never to take it seriously. Instead, I grab a fleece hoodie from the coat closet and shiver as I zip it over my "Hit like a girl" tee.

Yeah, I'm still wearing it. I was trying to save time by not changing shirts. Win some. Lose some. Although, every day with Erick feels like a win.

Myrtle's Diner is bustling with activity, and, for once, no one seems to notice as we enter and scoot toward our table.

My grandfather, Odell, opened this diner way back when he was married to my grandmother. When she still went by her birth name Myrtle. It wasn't until after her terrible accident in Europe and a stint in rehab that she emerged as Isadora, which had previously been her middle name. He's kept the diner afloat all these years and never changed the name. Now that he's one of a handful of people in the inner circle who know about the existence of Ghost-ma, he feels genuinely blessed.

Not to mention, we discovered a little of my psychic ability may have trickled down from his side of the family tree. It used to surprise me when he would deliver food to my table without me having to order. But now that my suspicions confirmed he's definitely a little psychic, it all makes sense. I love the touchstone of eating meals in this cozy, homey place. Back in the days of foster care, I never thought I'd have something like this in my life.

Erick and I slide onto opposite red-vinyl bench seats at the booth in the corner. The effervescent Tally sidles up and delivers two steaming mugs of black gold. "Morning. You two catch the game last night?"

There's nothing like the aroma of fresh coffee. "You betcha." No matter how many times I use the local phrase, it always makes me giggle. I love that I'm fitting into my new life, and my growing comfort with local jargon is just one of the many benefits.

"Well, that Atlas Hahn over at the Duds n' Suds owns the team, don't you know."

Atlas Hahn. So they weren't talking about Attila the Hun. Apparently, my psychic eavesdropping isn't as flawless as I'd like to imagine. "I actually *didn't* know. That launderette just opened, right?"

Tally nods her head and her flame-red topknot bobs with gossip glee. "Seems like six or eight months ago." She's definitely one of the key stops along the gossip super highway that runs through town.

I tilt my head with interest.

"Yeah. He's doing real good, dontcha know.

Folks all say we didn't need a laundromat, but sure seems like Mr. Hahn was right. My sister Tilly still works over at the bank, and she says they make big deposits every week. But you didn't hear it from me." She winks. "I better skedaddle."

With that, she turns and attends to her other customers. When I glance toward the kitchen, Odell offers a spatula salute through the red-Formica-trimmed orders-up window.

Our breakfasts are already underway. Less than five minutes later, Erick and I are nursing our second cups of coffee, having possibly overindulged at Final D, when Odell delivers the *pièce de résistance.*

Scrambled eggs with chorizo, home fries, an English muffin, and a bottle of Tabasco for me. A lovely stack of plate-size blueberry pancakes with several delicious sausages tucked along the side for Erick.

"How was the bout?"

"Didn't you go?" My shocked reply pushes its way past the bite of breakfast I'm enjoying. When it comes to hunger, manners take a back seat.

"Nah. Had to defrost the freezer and toss out some old inventory. Anne over at Bless Choux says that new health inspector is a real stickler, so I wanted to get my ducks in a row."

I've never understood the concept of getting

ducks in a row, but now's not the time. "Let me know if you need any help, Gramps."

He chuckles and gives my shoulder a squeeze. "I hear you're just about to log your final fifteen or twenty hours and get your actual PI license. I'm not gonna pull you away from that for some silly KP duty."

He and Erick share a chuckle. I have to assume that KP is some Army term that comes from their shared past. Not that they both served at the same time, by any stretch of the imagination, but they both served.

"Copy that."

While Erick and Odell discuss the finer points of last night's game, I inhale my breakfast. Call me crazy, but I enjoy eating my food when it's hot.

"Seems like those Rink Rashers are off to a good start. That's their third win, you know." Odell raps his knuckles twice on the silver-flecked Formica table and walks back to the kitchen.

"Should we head into the office after breakfast?" Erick shoves a large, syrupy bite of pancakes into his mouth and a little drop of 100% Canadian maple syrup glistens on his lower lip. It takes every ounce of self-control I don't possess to keep from leaping across the table and licking it off his face.

"Sure. Like my grandpa said, I'm so close I can almost taste it." Wink.

We finish our breakfast in silence, which honestly only takes about three more minutes, and as I'm sliding out of the booth to make good on my lost bet with Erick, his phone rings.

"I like a woman who keeps her word." He points to the cash in my hand and grabs his phone.

Tally tries to talk me out of paying, as is her custom, but I remind her that Odell has only promised me free *burgers and fries* for life, and breakfast doesn't fall into that category.

When I return to the table, Erick's face holds an expression that I've learned to read too well.

"Uh oh. Who died?"

CHAPTER 6

Detective Harper drains the last drops of coffee from his mug as he slides out of the booth. His voice is barely a whisper as he leans down. "Walk with me, Moon."

Outside, the crisp late winter morning seems somehow tainted as Erick relays the details of his phone call.

"Lars used his one phone call to call me."

"Lars? What do you mean, his 'one phone call'?"

"On her way to work this morning, Paulsen arrested him for murder."

If I could unhinge my jaw to let it literally hit the ground, I would. "Are you taking crazy pills over there? Who did Lars supposedly murder?"

"There was a hit-and-run last night. The victim,

a college student, died." Erick exhales his frustration in a slow, steady breath, squares his shoulders, and continues. "Lars had to meet a supplier this morning for an early delivery. When Paulsen drove past Final Destination, she noticed a van with a human-sized dent in the front and blood spray on the paint."

The size of my internal *gulp* has got to be visible.

"She stopped, confirmed that the van belonged to Lars, and slapped the handcuffs on him."

A movie-worthy montage of ten different scenarios flies through my mind, but not one of them involves the gentle giant Lars Nilsson hitting a human being and leaving them for dead. "That's insane. Lars would never do that. He would've called an ambulance or driven the victim to the hospital." My arms are waving like an inflatable tube man at a used car lot. "And when was he supposed to have done this? He was working the bar, right in front of our eyes, all night."

"That's part of the reason he called us. He told me he hit a deer on his way home last night. Lars needs someone to come in and convince Paulsen that she's barking up the wrong tree. He figured a former sheriff would be a solid character witness."

"What are we waiting for? Let's get over to the station and bust him out now." I make a quick about-face and head toward the holding cells. By the time Erick catches up and tugs at my arm, I'm halfway to the station.

"What's your plan, Moon? We just blast into the sheriff's station and demand his release? We aren't lawyers. Our word might count for something, but you know Paulsen. She'll want hard evidence." He shrugs. "I would've wanted the same. Not that I ever would've suspected Lars. But you know what I mean."

My brain is running circles around itself, searching for any type of useful idea. "I've got it!"

My husband rolls one hand over the other in a gesture meant to encourage me to move along.

"Find out where the accident happened and we'll find the deer. If we throw a dead deer on Paulsen's desk, that should get her attention."

Erick leans back in pleased surprise, but his head tilts and I know I've missed an important detail.

"Do you have any idea how much a full-grown deer weighs, Moon?"

"A hundred pounds?"

"Not even close. Easily two hundred to three hundred pounds. Not to mention, they're large. Very large. I'm pretty sure photographic evidence will be enough. And I still have that friend over at the lab. I'll give her a call and see if she has any results back on the blood on the van. It's pretty simple to identify if it's human or animal."

Lifting my left arm, I give him a celebratory hip bump. "Harper and Moon, on the case."

He chuckles and shakes his head as we pass the alley and approach the sheriff's station.

Erick holds the door for me. When I step through, Furious Monkeys, a.k.a. Deputy Baird, momentarily glances up from her screen, nods, and returns to the game for which I have nicknamed her. She bobs her head toward the back, and we push through the crooked wooden gate.

Mr. Harper dips his head in that way that insinuates he's doffing a cap as we pass by Deputy Gilbert.

Knowing my presence always puts Paulsen on the defensive, I pause and let Erick into the office first.

"Harper? What brings you in?"

When I take a step forward, her expression hardens. "Well, let me guess. Amateur snoop is here to try to spring Lars. Not gonna happen. I've got reports of a van fleeing the scene. That, combined with the huge dent and blood, is all the evidence I need." She scowls and her right hand takes a firmer grip on the handle of her holstered gun.

Erick nods, and my extrasensory perception,

fortunately, picks up on his plan to play his cards close to the vest.

"Understood, Paulsen. Simply here to have a little chat with Lars. I was his one phone call, and I need to check if he wants me to secure legal representation. I'm hoping you could do me that favor."

Surprisingly, the short, squat Sheriff Paulsen rises from her desk without protest. I back out of the office, and Erick makes way. She grabs the keys to the holding cells off the hook and silently leads us back to the thick metal security door separating those cells from the rest of the station.

The heavy door creaks as it swings open. Paulsen begrudgingly lets us pass.

Lars jumps to his feet. "Sheriff, I mean, Harper. Thanks for coming."

Paulsen mumbles something unsavory under her breath and continues to grumble as she exits the area.

Once the door slams behind her, I hurry to the bars and lean in. "Do you need anything? Do you want me to bring you some breakfast from the diner?"

"Nah. I had a full Swedish breakfast before I left the house this morning. My late wife never used to let me leave without eating. Are you guys gonna get me out of here?"

The six-foot-seven man has never looked so helpless.

Erick nods an affirmative. "I need to know where you hit that deer, Lars. Mitzy and I will head out and get pictures. Plus, I'm gonna call in a favor from the lab. I think we'll have you out of here by noon. Will that work?"

The tension in Lars's shoulders evaporates, and his enormous frame exhales relief. "I don't care if it takes you a week, eh? Just get me out of here."

Lars relays the particulars about when and where he hit the deer. But just as we're about to leave, he adds a troubling detail.

"Thing is, I didn't see him flop in the ditch, you know? Looked to me like it headed into the tree line. I didn't realize how hard I'd hit it until I got home and saw the dent in the front of my van."

The hairs on the back of my neck prickle to attention, and I sense a similar concern from my husband. Since his inner hero has a serious issue with stretching the truth, I leap to his rescue. "Don't worry, Lars. We'll find it and get the proof we need." Then, using a phrase I neither understand nor endorse, I offer the only comfort I have in my tiny bag of tricks. "Sit tight. We'll take care of it."

Pressing the buzzer on the door brings an angry sheriff to set us free. The overall vibe definitely indicates her strong preference is to keep us all in a holding cell.

Erick nods his thanks as we continue silently past the interrogation rooms toward the bullpen.

Paulsen can't leave well enough alone. "You two stay out of this. We got an open and shut case, and I don't need amateurs mucking it up, eh?" She runs her tongue over her top teeth and makes an impatient squeaking noise.

Erick maintains his cool. Unfortunately, I wasn't born that way.

"Don't worry, Paulsen. I don't think the folks in Pin Cherry Harbor will consider solving this case 'mucking it up.'"

I shove through the swinging gate and make my exit before Sherrif Crabby Pants has a comeback.

Outside, Erick chuckles under his breath.

"You're getting the hang of it, aren't you, Harper? She never wanted to be sheriff to serve the people. She only wanted the power. After everything you did for her when you were sheriff — treating her with respect she didn't deserve — this is the thanks you get."

He slips an arm around my shoulders and pulls me close as we walk toward home and transportation. "Treating people with respect isn't something you do because you're expecting anything in return. It's just the way my mama raised me."

I snake my arm around his waist and give him a squeeze. "Well, I'm not going to argue with Gracie Harper, *Ricky*. She raised the best man I've ever known. So, I'll take your word for it." Using his mother's nickname for him always lightens the mood.

He gently kisses the top of my head as we approach the garage. He taps in the code and the door rolls up.

"We're taking my Jeep?"

"Yeah, you heard where Lars said he hit that deer. I'm not taking my baby on those roads."

"Wow, Harper. I never realized that I ranked below your precious Nova in importance."

He refuses to take the bait. "Hop in, Moon. Clearly, you have no idea where we're going."

"You got it, boss. Will this little jacket be enough? Do I need a hat or mittens?"

He tugs on his army surplus jacket. "This is what I'm wearing. I'm pretty sure you'll be okay."

"Copy that."

Grabbing his mobile phone, he places a call to the lab. "Hey, Roxy. It's Harper."

I remember how jealous I was when I first met Roxborough. I didn't understand that Roxy was a nickname. I thought Erick was flirting with her. Despite my status as his official wife, there's still a thread of concern tickling my heart.

"Hey, Moon. Did you hear me?"

"Yeeeesss." My shaky voice betrays me.

He chuckles. "Roxy is gonna run the test. The van is in impound, and the tech already gathered evidence."

As he follows the directions Lars provided, the roads indeed get narrower and more rural. Eventually, we're rumbling down washboard gravel roads, and I can understand why he was hesitant to bring his beautifully restored muscle car on this trip.

My Jeep, on the other hand, is built for this stuff.

"Keep your eyes peeled, Moon. If Lars is right about the deer entering the tree line, we're looking for broken branches or tracks in the snow. Anything you can see — or sense — would be a big help."

"I'll watch my side of the road. You watch yours." Surely, there's no reason to look ahead, as we haven't passed another car for almost twenty minutes.

Reaching out with my psychic senses, I attempt to remain open to any information that might trickle in. Wouldn't you know—

Pain like a thunderbolt hits me in the gut, and my arms ache as though they've been crushed under a bulldozer.

A strangled scream escapes, and Erick slams on the brakes. "What is it? Are you okay?"

"There. Right over there."

He scans the ditch and identifies tracks leaving the roadway and something dark on the snow.

"You better stay here, Moon. Looks like the animal has been badly injured. If it's still alive, it could be aggressive."

"Are you nuts, Harper? I'm not gonna let you disappear into the woods where some crazed animal is loose. I'm gonna follow you with my phone at the ready. We can handle this together. Remember, it's Harper AND Moon Investigations. Not Harper the Hero Investigations."

He glances across the vehicle at me and smirks. "You gotta admit, Harper the Hero Investigations has a nice ring to it."

"Touché." He always knows how to make me laugh.

We exit the vehicle and head toward the bare tree line on the opposite side of the road.

I've been allowed to come along, but there's no way he's letting me out front. He motions for me to fall in line behind him as he follows the blood trail.

Sorry to mention that part, but it's the only way we can track this poor wounded animal.

As we enter the dappled sunlight and deep shade of the birch-and-pine forest, a low moaning reaches my ears first and then Harper's.

"I hear it. Follow me."

We head toward the mournful bellowing and, in about a hundred yards, we stumble upon the injured buck.

Erick turns, and his gaze is impenetrable. "Head back to the car, Moon. No questions. Are we clear?"

I haven't heard his official voice in some time, and I have to admit it does the trick. "Yes, sir."

He walks slowly toward the poor animal.

I wish I could turn off my psychic senses, but I left them wide open to help the search. A flood of compassion and resignation flows from my husband and hits me as I rush toward the Jeep.

One word floats through the ether.

Gun.

Jumping in the vehicle, I close off my abilities like Silas taught me, and plug my ears.

Erick silently returns.

The muscles in his jaw clench as he opens the driver's door. "That was tough. Both of his front legs had compound fractures. It was the only thing I could do."

Tears are streaming down my face. Not because he did anything wrong, but because I can feel how difficult it was for him to do what had to be done.

"You did the right thing. As hard as it . . . "

"Thanks, Moon." He sniffs sharply and climbs in. "I took the pictures we need for evidence."

Reaching over the center console, I grip his hand. "I'm glad we found him. I'm sorry you—"

Erick squeezes my hand. "It's never easy. I wish deer didn't ever get hit." He exhales gruffly. "Comes with the territory at the latitude." He shakes his head and gives my hand one last pat before turning the key.

CHAPTER 7

THE SOMBER DRIVE BACK to town is almost more than I can bear. When the ringing of his phone breaks the tense silence, I exhale the breath I didn't realize I've been holding.

"Harper . . .

"Okay. Okay. You sure? I owe you, Roxy."

He drops the phone in his lap and utters a sigh of relief.

"Was it good news?"

Erick reaches across and takes my hand. "Roxy confirmed the blood on the van was animal. With that and the evidence we—" He's unable to complete the sentence.

"Thanks for helping Lars, Harper."

Back in town, we park on the opposite side of the street, in front of the boarded-up Montgomery

Wards. For the first time in months, I see Main Street for what it is. Half abandoned. Desperate for someone or something to breathe new life.

It's funny how those things fade into the background once you fall in love with a place. To me, the town always seems alive, friendly, welcoming. I suppose that's the vibe that brings tourists to all the festivals.

In fact, next weekend is the Memorial Curling Open. I can't believe I'm thinking this, but I need to solve this case before the festivities kick off so Erick and I can enjoy the games.

When we reenter the station, roughly an hour after our previous visit, Deputy Baird has vacated her post for reasons known only to her, and the bullpen is empty. Erick strides through the station as though he were the sheriff. Stopping in the bullpen, I hang back and let him deliver the *coup de grâce.*

"I'm sure you heard from Roxy. That's animal blood on Mr. Nilsson's van. And I have photos of the deer he hit. Happy to give you the location if you want to drive out there yourself to confirm."

Creeping forward, I push my way through the swinging wooden gate and walk past the lonely metal desks in their crooked rows, with their messy stacks of paper and random coffee stains. I have to get a better vantage point.

He calls up the photos on his phone and tosses it on her desk. Covering my mouth with my hand, I stifle a chuckle. I gotta say, I love Harper the Hero.

She gets to her feet, which isn't a long trip, and her right hand rests firmly on the grip of her pistol. "Don't try to throw your weight around in here. I'm the sheriff of Birch County. Not you."

And then the world seems to stop spinning. If not for my psychic replay, I might not believe what I hear.

"I think it's time to put this charade to an end, don't you, Paulsen? Consider yourself notified you won't be running unopposed this November." Erick retrieves his phone, points to the holding cell keys, and steps back.

Paulsen is red in the face and fuming, but unable to speak. She snatches the keys from the hook and, a moment later, a grateful Lars Nilsson appears. He lumbers toward Erick and crushes him in a bear hug. I pray for my safety and hope I'm not next.

What's the saying, wish in one hand and—? Lars constricts me in his arms and repeats his unending gratitude.

"Free drinks for life, Moon. Free drinks for life."

Now, if you know Lars, you know what an amazing gesture this is. When I worked my undercover gig as a waitress at Final D, he made me pay for any drinks I spilled and he wouldn't let me keep my tips because I wasn't an actual employee.

Erick offers to give him a ride to the bar and tells him he'll talk to Skeeter, the local mechanic, about towing the van out of the impound yard and back to Final D — no charge.

Paulsen is grumbling something about paperwork, but the three of us march out of the sheriff's station as the victorious Three Musketeers.

Five minutes later, standing in the parking lot at Final Destination, twiddling my thumbs, a sudden concern bubbles to the surface. "Now that we got Lars released, are we still on the case?"

Erick nods without hesitation. "I don't like Paulsen's attitude. We should go to the scene and see if we stumble on anything she missed."

After scoffing openly, I step closer and grab his hand with both of mine. "Are we gonna talk about what you said? You know, about November?"

The muscles in his jaw tighten and release. He drags his left thumb along the hint of stubble as he exhales.

I rush to smooth things over. "You don't have to talk about it. It just surprised me. You know?"

Gently twisting his hand from my grip, he rakes his fingers through slicked-back blond hair, loosening a little swath of long bangs that drape across his face as he gazes down at me. "I was out of line. I should've talked to you first. I've been going back and forth for months."

Not having the ability to hide my shock, I blurt out the first thing that pops into my head. "Months? We've only been at this gig for two years. Are you saying you've been regretting it for most of that time?"

His face instantly washes over with shock and apologies. "No! I love every minute of working cases together. But I miss the day-to-day. The connection with my community that being the sheriff provided. I know it's strange. And I'm sure I'm not explaining it very well. But—"

Pressing a single finger to his pouty mouth, I gaze up at him with what I hope translates as all the admiration in my heart. "You don't have to explain anything to me. One of the reasons I fell in love with you was because of your dedication to justice and this community. If you want to run in the November election, I know a very wealthy heiress who will gladly back your campaign."

He scoops his arms around me and kisses me with the kind of wild abandon that can lead to places we don't have time to go. Wriggling free, I brush my hair back and attempt to get the full-body tingles under control. "Well, um, you said something about visiting the scene?"

I'm pleased to see that he appears equally breathless. "Uh, yeah. That's what I said."

He opens the passenger door of the jeep, and the heat from his body nearly singes me as I slip past to climb into the vehicle.

When we arrive at the back of the gymnasium at the community college, rows of yellow crime-scene tape block our way.

Erick pulls to the side and parks. As we approach the barrier of plastic, he glances at a gap between two of the stanchions. "Looks like it's okay to walk through there."

"Erick No Middle Name Harper. If I didn't know better, I'd say you're looking for a loophole. Stay in your lane!"

A deep chuckle rumbles from his chest, and we step through the gap to see what we can see.

Unfortunately, the scene of the accident is all too easy to locate.

"Why don't you keep to the edges, Moon, and see if you can suss out any of the less obvious evidence?"

For once, he'll get no argument from me. Hugging the edge of the two-tone brick structure, I reach out with my psychic senses, and even beg my uncooperative mood ring to throw me a bone.

Nada. Bupkus.

Continuing toward the rear door and the adjacent storage container, I attempt to trigger a possible psychometry hit by touching the door handle and the large lever that locks into place to secure the shipping container.

Some innocuous images of derby girls entering, exiting, and loading stacks of portable flooring are my only reward.

Sticking to the edges, I start a return trip along the curb and evergreen hedge bordering this access area.

As I approach Erick's position, he gets to his feet and joins me. "That's it for me. I need to see if Deputies Gilbert or Johnson will leak anything. I'm making an assumption about the rate of speed required to end a life, and I just can't see anyone coming in that hot."

"What do you mean?"

He gestures to the roped-off area. "It's a dead end, Moon. If the driver was pulling out, there's no way a van could get up enough speed to be a killing machine in the twenty feet between the storage container and the site of impact. If they were coming the other direction, from the parking lot, what possible reason would the driver have for such a high rate of speed? There's nowhere to go. Barely enough time to brake before hitting that solid steel storage container. This was no accident."

At the moment I'm about to chime in with my

thoughts on the suspected murder, my mood ring jumps to life.

My finger is encircled with a fiery heat that immediately draws my attention to the smoky grey stone. The mist clears, and a strange image solidifies. Tightly wrapped plastic bundles. I lean down for a closer look.

"Are you getting something, Moon? What is it?"

"They're packets. Wrapped in—"

"Pills or powder?"

I hold my hand toward Erick as though he can see the images in my ring.

"Hey, this is your area. See if you can get a closer look."

"Right." Pulling the ring in for an inspection of the image provides little help. "It looks like pills or — chunks? But it's hard to tell. Does it make a difference?"

"As you know, we put a pretty huge dent in the counterfeit opioid trade when we took down Ivy and her gang. However, the vacuum left by those arrests has probably allowed some new players to infiltrate. Most likely methamphetamine, crystal meth. If the rumors are true, it's definitely getting out of hand."

He pulls me close and steers me back through the gap in the stanchions.

"You want a chocolate croissant?"

"Now who's the psychic?" The session with the mood ring drained me, and I definitely need a kick of something to recover and continue on the case. "Let's head to the patisserie. I could use some of Anne's magical hot chocolate, too."

Deep in thought, Erick drives slowly. Since I've promised not to use my psychic abilities on him, I can only guess at what's going on inside that head of his. Ninety percent of it is likely related to this case, but that remaining ten percent is planning his campaign strategy.

No judgment. I knew from the moment he resigned that he missed the force. He's a born leader. A group guy. The deputies respect him and look up to him as a role model. Erick was great for Birch County. He always put the citizens first. He has never been a glory seeker. Always a dedicated public servant. If that's what his calling is, I'm not gonna stand in his way.

I can get my PI hours in before he wins the election and heads back to the sheriff's station. Plus, I'll totally keep the name of the agency, even if I'm the only one running it. Technically, I am both a Harper and a Moon.

"Earth to Moon." He chuckles at his joke. "We're here. You want me to grab something to go, or are we heading in?"

I'm out of the car in a flash. "After you, soon-to-be sheriff."

His head hangs under the weight of embarrass-ment, but I feel hope swell within him.

Yep. We're gonna make this happen.

Inside Bless Choux, the luscious aromas of hot pastry and indulgent fillings envelop me. When Erick veers off, I honestly have no idea why. How-ever, as I approach the counter, the sight of a tan uniform, and the unmistakable thick neck and black hair definitely belong to Deputy Johnson.

Erick approaches the counter and pats the young deputy on the back. "Johnson, you draw the short straw today? They send you on a doughnut run?"

His cheeks redden, and he looks down at the counter. "Nah. I'm supposed to be cruising up and down the streets looking for another damaged van. Pretty frustrating assignment. I just needed a little pick me up."

My husband offers one more pat of cncourage-ment and turns his attention to the proprietor. "How you doing, Anne?"

"Not too bad, Sheriff. Shoot! I just can't get used to it. I meant to say, Erick. How about you?"

He leans in. "Can you two keep a secret?"

Anne's eyes nearly pop out of her head. Deputy Johnson shrugs. No one in this town can keep a secret. The whole place would grind to a halt if the gossip stopped flowing.

Erick lowers his voice, and I have to click on my psychic hearing to pick up the message he delivers. "I've decided to run in November."

Anne claps her hands with sheer joy, and Deputy Johnson places both of his large hands on the counter and breathes an enormous sigh of relief.

"You've got my vote, Sheriff."

Anne eagerly chimes in. "Mine too. And whatever you want is on the house today!"

Erick waves away the offer. "Nonsense. I can't be taking bribes. Not a good optic. On the other hand, I can certainly do my local law enforcement a favor. How about you box up a couple dozen of whatever the deputy prefers and I'll pick up the tab."

It appears as though Deputy Johnson might shed a tear. "This is why we all miss you, sir."

The emotion is getting far too thick. Time for me to stir the pot.

"Mind if I have a word with Deputy Johnson while Anne puts his order together?"

Erick opens his mouth, closes it firmly, and arches an eyebrow before he replies. "As you may have guessed, my wife will continue to run the PI office."

Johnson cracks a genuine smile and nods his

head. "I wouldn't have it any other way. My pops always says she's got a gift from the Lord himself."

If you don't remember, Johnson's father is pastor of the First Methodist Church and seems to have an inkling that I'm a little extra normal. He has, of course, assigned these traits to the higher power of his own choosing.

Johnson and I head to a bistro table, and he pulls out a chair for me.

"I sure could use a little help on this case, Johnson. How about a swap of information?"

He squares his shoulders. "Tell you what, if you have something we don't have, I'll reciprocate."

May as well hit him with everything I've got. "How is the trafficking of methamphetamines involved?"

The color drains from the deputy's face. He pushes back from the table, and his Adam's apple struggles to swallow. "That hasn't been released to the press. It's just a hypothesis Deputy Gilbert threw out. Paulsen squashed it like a bug."

"I'm here to tell you it's connected. I don't know how yet, but it is." Leaning forward and flashing my eyebrows, I say, "Now, what do you have for me?"

He glances around the bakery and leans forward. "Truth is, there's been an uptick in drug-related crime. Seems like there's a new player in town. But we've got nothing solid."

"10-4. If I figure out the connection, you'll be the second to know, Johnson."

He nods his gratitude, and I continue. "What about the manner of death?" Now it's my turn to struggle with swallowing and brace for impact.

"Definitely hit-and-run. Definitely vehicular. Not to be indelicate, Miss, but practically every rib in the young man's body was broken, as well as both femurs. Official cause of death is internal hemorrhage."

A shiver shakes my body, and I rub my hands over my face. "How terrible. His poor family."

Johnson nods soberly. "Yeah. Gilbert drew the short straw on that one. He's gotta drive out there today. I s'pose cruising the streets looking for a smashed van isn't so bad compared to the alternative."

Erick arrives and hands Johnson a large pink pastry box. "Here you go, Deputy. Thanks for your support."

Johnson hops out of his chair and offers it to Erick. "Have a seat, Sheriff."

"Easy. I haven't won yet."

Johnson laughs openly. "It's going to be a landslide, sir. If it's all the same to you, I'm gonna go ahead and start practicing."

The flush of joy that washes over my husband is palpable. Good thing I'm an independent, self-reliant woman. Some gals might be scared to run an investigative agency on their own. I'm kinda looking forward to the competition.

Johnson tilts his head in my direction. "Thanks for the information, Miss."

"Same." I display a lame thumbs-up.

Once he exits to the street, I bring Erick up to speed on what I was able to glean from the deputy.

Erick presses his lips firmly together and seems simultaneously satisfied and disappointed. "I knew it was no accident. Nobody suffers that much bodily damage from an accidental, low-speed hit-and-run. It was definitely murder. And we're absolutely on the case."

With images of the shattered lives of the boy's parents swimming in my head, I'm unable to muster the necessary enthusiasm to chant our catchphrase. Regardless, my husband is right. There's no way we're letting this murderer walk free.

CHAPTER 8

Lucky for us, the overzealous Sheriff Paulsen keeps giving us reasons to double our efforts.

After parking in the garage, Erick's phone rings while we trudge from the alley beside my bookshop to our PI office a couple blocks away. He holds up a finger and jogs back toward the alley to take the call.

My internal snoop can't take the suspense. I poke my head around the corner, and Erick motions for me to join him as he puts the call on speaker.

"Look, man, Beryl, that's my gal, told Paulsen the damage to her van happened months ago. Paulsen even admitted the red substance might not be blood, but she refused to release Beryl and the other gals until the lab techs complete their final analysis. Can you help me out, bro?"

"Happy to help. Where's the van now?"

Boomer scoffs. "Paulsen wouldn't say. But I know people, you know? It's at the impound yard. Techs are done collecting evidence, but I couldn't get it released."

"No worries. Skeeter's got an all-access pass." They share a knowing grunt and end the conversation.

Erick makes a quick call. Skeeter promises to check out the damage as soon as possible and report back.

Throwing my hands in the air, I take a swipe at the easy target of Sheriff Paulsen. "Are you telling me she thinks these derby teams took their fight to the street, and someone was killed?"

"No idea. Boomer swears Beryl wasn't involved. She drove the Slammer Jammers' team van directly back to Broken Rock, and there's a record of her sending an email at 10:30 p.m."

"She could have sent that from her phone. From anywhere." My face betrays my doubt.

"I said the same thing." Our eyes meet, and the unspoken thought that great minds think alike hangs for a moment between us. "Before you joined the call, Boomer said she didn't have her phone, though. She never takes her phone to a bout. Something about wanting to stay focused pregame . . . Anyway, her roommate can verify that the phone was at their apartment in Broken Rock all evening."

"What if Beryl isn't telling the truth, though? Do you even know her?"

My hubby shakes his head. "Nope. But I know Boomer. And I know he's always had my back, and he's never lied to me. So, if he needs my help, he's got it."

My shoulders shrug of their own free will. "It's not the best alibi. But assuming it's the truth, why doesn't he investigate this himself?"

Erick stops in the middle of the sidewalk and turns toward me. All residue of the "great minds" link-up has vanished.

Oops. I'm not sure whether it's a psychic vibe or common sense, but I can read his expression like an open book. "Right. He's the boyfriend. Not necessarily objective."

My hubby takes a comic bow. "My Queen."

Oh brother. Punching him playfully on the shoulder, we continue toward our office on First Avenue.

"How long till Skeeter—"

RING. RING.

Erick grabs his phone. "I hope you didn't break any speed limits getting there that fast." They share a chuckle as he taps the speaker icon.

"I was already here. After I dropped off the van

at Final D, I towed a car from the fire lane at the high school. Got a couple of those fancy pants moms from The Pines who think the red curb doesn't apply to them."

Everyone in town is familiar with the upper-crust inhabitants of the high-end Pines planned community.

Erick dives into collecting information. "What's the scoop on Beryl's van?"

"I'm no crime tech, Harper, but that damage is fresh. Maybe not last night fresh, but it can't be more than a week old. The exposed metal is shiny as a new hubcap, and there are still a few pieces of broken headlight wedged behind the bumper. You and I both know those would be long gone if this accident had happened months ago."

"Thanks, Skeeter." Erick glances toward me, shakes his head, and bites his lower lip. "What about the blood?"

"That's a big negatory. It's something red. Not paint. But not blood. Want me to taste it?"

Without thinking, I shout, "What? No!"

"Hiya, Mitzy. Don't worry. It's the best way to identify a substance. I been doing it my whole life and I'm still here." There's a pause, followed by the sound of Skeeter smacking his lips. "Hmmm, tastes like sugar. Karo syrup, to be exact."

Once again, I butt in. "That's what they use to make fake blood for the movies."

Erick and I exchange a "more on this later" look, and he signs off. "Thanks, Skeeter. I'll update Boomer and see what he knows about this fake blood."

Before Erick can place the call, I grab his arm and sigh loudly. "The red food coloring! Pye knew about the fake blood."

He pats my hand and shakes his head. "Impressive. If that cat could talk, he might take over the world."

Scoffing, I hold up a warning finger. "Don't give him any ideas."

"I better call Boomer." He waits for my nod and grabs his phone.

"Hey, buddy, I just got an update from Skeeter. You happen to know if Beryl was involved in making some kind of amateur film?"

Boomer adamantly denies any such involvement, but then he stops in the middle of his protest and laughs out loud. "Hold on. Her and some of her teammates were shooting some super-aggressive footage for the team website. She said fans love the blood and guts of it all."

I arch an eyebrow, but Erick immediately accepts the explanation. "Well, that explains the fake blood. Thing is, that dent in her car is fresh. When did that really happen?"

Boomer exhales. "No idea. I'll swing by lockup and see if she can explain it. You know how Paulsen gets with suspects . . . Beryl probably got scared and lied about the damage. Maybe she hit something when they recorded that derby footage. You still think she's innocent, though, right?"

Erick glances at me for a moment, and I wobble my head from side to side, not sure what I believe.

"Jury's still out, bro. How about you give us an update as soon as you have one?"

"10-4." Boomer ends the call, and Erick slowly pushes his phone into his pocket. His face is a mask of conflicting emotions.

Ignoring my issues with the flimsy alibi and the sketchy story, I attempt to switch into sleuthing mode. "All right. Assuming Boomer's girlfriend is innocent, what other suspects do we have?"

Erick throws his arms in the air as he exhales. "Anybody in Pin Cherry driving a van last night — except Lars. It doesn't even have to be someone who attended the game. The hit-and-run occurred well after the spectators had cleared out. The Rink Rashers, and the few Slammer Jammers that hung around to help, were disassembling the portable track and loading it into the storage container behind the gymnasium. Boomer said the community college gives them free storage in exchange for an annual exhibition match fundraiser."

"That's cool."

"It is. But it still implicates skaters. Specifically, whoever was driving the van. Trouble is, they're a tightlipped group. Boomer said Sheriff Paulsen couldn't get any details from the four she took in."

Stopping at the bottom of the steps leading to our office door, I press a hand to my chest in mock surprise. "What? The friendly, charismatic Sheriff Paulsen didn't receive cooperation?"

Despite his usual ability to remain neutral, Erick chuckles. "You're right. Paulsen isn't exactly delicate with people she suspects of murder. I was thinking maybe we could head over to the practice warehouse and chat with the skaters."

Skipping up to the top step, I turn and waggle my eyebrows. "Or—"

His expression turns stoic, and the color drains from his handsome cheeks. "Don't say it, Moon. That is not a good idea."

"Come on. Stop playing psychic. You have no idea what I was going to say."

As I take a breath and prepare to elaborate, he steps closer, and his steel-blue eyes bore into my soul. "I'm willing to bet you're about to suggest going undercover in the roller derby league. Which is a terrible idea for a number of reasons, but here are the top two: 1. Your adorable lack of coordination would make it seriously difficult to impress seasoned roller derby girls; 2. The hit-and-run was definitely not an accident. We're looking for a murderer."

Maybe there's a part of me that genuinely enjoys flirting with danger. Maybe it's leftover from my misspent youth, or maybe I'm a secret adrenaline junkie. "Tell you what, Harper. If I can pick this lock" — I point to the front door of our office — "in under thirty seconds. I get to go undercover. If not, I'll listen to whatever your lame, boring Plan B might be."

He glances at the deadbolt and smirks. "I spec'd out that lock, Moon. I don't care what kind of juvenile delinquent you claim to be. There's no way you can do it in under thirty seconds. You're on." He extends his right hand. I grip it firmly and shake. "Deal."

He whips out his phone, taps the timer, and shouts, "Go!"

Dropping to one knee, I slip my lock pick and the tension wrench from my pocket. Yes, I pretty much always carry them. A girl never knows.

As soon as I wiggle the lock pick into the plug, a moment of doubt washes over me. This is a good lock. This could be too much for me to handle. Nope! I gotta push these doubts out of my mind.

Collecting all of my abilities, including the extra ones, I focus like a laser beam on my task.

Click. Click. Click. The first three pins easily move above the shear line.

"Fifteen seconds." Erick sounds too pleased with himself.

The fourth pin is tricky. I have to release a little tension to move it up and then put more tension on. By the time I reach the seventh pin, Erick sounds off the final countdown and my chest tightens.

"Two—"

"I'm in!"

CHAPTER 9

"How did you do that? I was sure I had you beat on this one." Erick looks genuinely disappointed.

Getting to my feet, I push my lock pick back into my pocket, inhale sharply, and gaze up at my partner. "Never underestimate me, Harper."

"Touché, Moon. Touché."

Pushing open the door for Erick, I wave my arm in a grand gesture. "I'll leave you to it here at the office. I've got other work to do."

He stops on the threshold, near enough to give my heart a couple of extra thumps.

"Where are you going? You're so close to getting all of your PI hours. I thought you were working in the office today?"

"No way! I've got to get back to the bookshop,

set up the murder board, and see if Grams has any video of her roller derby days. I'm kind of a visual learner. I need to get more information uploaded to the ol' psychic replay bank. Plus, I'm going to need a miracle from Silas. He's gotta have something in his magic alchemy chest — don't tell him I said magic — that will help me on the coordination front."

Despite Erick's objection to the plan, his expression carries excitement and a ripple of pride. "It's not that I don't have faith in Silas Willoughby's arcane knowledge, but turning you into a legitimate roller derby player may be a bridge too far."

Pushing to my tiptoes, I gaze up at my husband and mutter, "Oh, ye of little faith."

He rewards me with a soft kiss, and I rush down the steps, nearly tripping, giggle softly, and head for the bookshop.

Entering through the heavy metal door leading from the alleyway to the back room, I'm not surprised to find my volunteer employee, Twiggy, hard at work.

"Where you been, kid? I'm about to put in the weekly order. You need any more tacks or green yarn for that murder board you're always playing with?"

Twiggy slowly turns in her dilapidated rolly chair like a black-and-white horror movie reveal.

One biker-boot-clad foot is kicked up on the opposite knee of her standard dungarees. Her grey pixie cut looks freshly trimmed. Not professionally, mind you. It's definitely something she's handled herself.

"Did you get a haircut?"

Her foot slides off her knee and stomps to the floor. "Focus up, kid. You need the yarn or not?"

"Yeah. I need the yarn. We just got a case."

"Yup. I heard about that hit-and-run. I figured you guys would be all over it. You know that kid was on his way to big things."

"What kid?"

The look on Twiggy's face manages to somehow condescend and ooze sympathy simultaneously. "I thought you said you took the case, doll. What kind of private investigator doesn't bother to find out who the victim is before they take a case?"

Since I'm fresh out of snappy comebacks, I simply swallow once and offer a version of the truth. "We just put ourselves on the case, like fifteen minutes ago." A mild exaggeration, but she doesn't know that. "I haven't had time to do any investigating. I ran back here to get set for my undercover gig."

There's no need for me to explain what I plan to do undercover. Twiggy's patronizing cackle echoes off the walls of the small back room and manages to bring Grams swooping into the fray.

"All right. Enough laughter at my expense. I think I've paid your fee for the day. Now, tell me more about the victim."

Twiggy struggles to get herself under control as Grams fires questions. The hilarious antics of my life are the only form of payment Twiggy will accept for her work at my bookstore. The Bell, Book & Candle would be nothing without her, so I can hardly begrudge her this moment of amusement.

While my volunteer employee catches her breath, I bring Grams up to speed on what I know about the hit-and-run — and my plans to go undercover.

"Oh, sweetie, the 3 x 5 cards for your murder wall can wait. We best call Silas at once. I can show you all the video in the universe, but unless he can keep you steady on your skates, you're doomed. Those gals gobble up fresh meat like a pack of ravenous wolves."

"Fresh meat?"

Grams presses the back of her hand to her forehead like a Victorian woman about to make use of a fainting couch. "First, call Silas. Then we'll get to all of your questions."

Twiggy takes a deep breath, and I cross my arms, preparing for another assault on my coordination.

"So, the kid was Jason Samson. Born and raised

in Pin Cherry. His family has always struggled. He's got a younger sister in a full-time care facility. His father was injured on the docks and drinks away his disability check every month. The mom used to work two custodial jobs to pay for the care expenses, but I hear she's taken a job as the night manager at that new laundromat."

"Wow. That's rough. This Jason, he's a kid? Who would run down a kid on purpose? It has to be an accident."

"I'm sure you're right. He was in his third year at the community college. Finished his first Associate's and was getting some additional credits before he transferred to university. He was student body president or some kind of thing. You'll find out. Near as I could tell, from what I heard around town, he was loved by all. The exact opposite of his father."

"Thanks, Twiggy. That's a big help." An awkward silence fills the back room. "I better call Silas and see what he's got up his sleeve, and then I'll reach out to Erick with the information about the victim."

"Come up to the apartment, sweetie. I'll show you where the old tapes are."

Grams vanishes through the wall, and I step out of the back room and walk down the hallway toward the spiral staircase — like a civilized human.

The enormous chandelier suspended from the tin-plated ceiling glistens as sunbeams illuminate the dust moats floating softly throughout the bookshop. Not wanting to send Twiggy into another fit of giggles, I carefully climb over the "No Admittance" chain at the bottom of the spiral staircase and softly make my way up the metal treads to the mezzanine. Placing my hands on the curved balustrade of the Rare Books Loft and gazing over the bookshop always brings a grateful grin to my face. This place is magical. Every book, able to transport its reader to another place. A place that exists only when they live in those pages. But somehow, the memory remains long after they file the tome away on their own bookshelf. What is magic really, if not the ability to create these feelings and emotions?

Oops. Better not let Silas catch me talking about magic.

With that, I grab my phone and press the number for *Secret Alchemist* in my contacts. Turning on my best manners, I wait for my mentor to answer. Grams swirls around me. "Put it on speaker!"

I do as I'm told.

"Good morning, Mizithra."

Wow, formal name territory and I haven't even asked my favor. "Good morning, Mr. Willoughby.

Would you have time in your schedule to stop by the bookshop today?"

A soft chuckle emanates from the phone, and I can easily picture him smoothing his bushy grey mustache with a thumb and forefinger.

"Indeed. You have chosen to take the case of Jason Samson?"

"Actually, we're working for the defense on this one. You remember that Deputy from Broken Rock, Boomer?"

"Indeed. Continue."

"Paulsen arrested his girlfriend. Boomer claims she has an alibi and had nothing to do with this terrible accident."

"Your use of the word accident implies you've already uncovered evidence to support your hypothesis."

Attempting to keep my grumble at an inaudible level, I have to admit he's caught me misspeaking. "I've had the case for less than a day. It seems pretty likely it was a murder, based on some stuff Erick and I uncovered. I don't have enough information to even make up a hypothesis. But I do know the derby players are tightlipped, and the only way I'm going to get any information—"

"I shall make my way to the bookstore posthaste. If you're planning on finishing that sentence in the manner I surmise, you shall require all the help I can muster. Sit tight."

The call ends and, for the millionth time, I throw one hand on my curvy hip and sigh. "What does that even mean to 'sit tight'? And how would one do such a thing?"

Grams snickers and phases through the wall of books into the hidden apartment.

CHAPTER 10

BEFORE FOLLOWING GHOST-MA, I take a moment to appreciate what I have. Scanning the beautifully curved mezzanine and its massive collection of arcane tomes, I breathe in the possibility of endless worlds. The oak reading desks are perfectly aligned, as usual, and each of the green glass lampshades stands ready for action. Striding across the thick hand-knotted rug, I reach up to the candle sconce that serves as the handle for the secret doorway, tilt it down, and gaze fondly at my ancient copy of *Saducismus Triumphatus* as the door slides open.

When I step into the apartment, Grams is already failing to open the hidden drawer.

"I got it, Grams."

I give the long drawer below the built-in bookcase a solid push, and it pops open and reveals rows of old VHS tapes. If I hadn't attended film school and learned the history of moving pictures, I'm pretty sure I'd have no idea what I was looking at. Once again, the strange loops of my personal history weave together to support my perfect present.

"Where should I start?"

Grams points to the third tape down in the second row. "This is a great one. Start here!" She clutches one of her many strands of pearls and literally glows as she waits for me to cue up the tape.

The announcer's voice is muffled by all the background noise, but we can make out most of his comments.

"Tipsy Kitty cuts through the pack like a hot knife through butter. She grabs lead jammer status and heads around the track to score as many points as possible for the Birch County Banshees."

The crowd roars to life as Tipsy Kitty overtakes members of the Disco Darlings. Hands waving in the air temporarily block the camera.

"It looks like Sister Sledgehammer will take her out with a deadly hip check. Oh! Tipsy Kitty throws a spin move, avoids the blocker, and scores two more points for the Banshees!"

Hitting pause on the remote, I glance toward Ghost-ma and shake my head. "I don't know how you did it, Grams! You were unstoppable. I thought I inherited my clumsiness from you. What gives?"

Myrtle Isadora shrugs her translucent shoulders, and her burial gown flutters in an unseen breeze. She thoughtfully spins one of her wedding rings and tilts her head back and forth as the memories sift through her ethereal brain like seeds through a rain stick. "I don't remember ever feeling clumsy on the track. It was the one place in my life I felt in control. Plus, I never drank before a bout." She hangs her head and exhales slowly. "Of course, I drank plenty after. Just one of many alcohol-induced regrets. There were probably a few people I forgot about when I was on Step Nine — making amends."

"You did the best you could at the time, Grams. And I think it's awesome that roller derby was so empowering for you. I kinda wish I had a thing like that."

Ghost-ma floats several inches higher, and her shimmering aura intensifies with saturated colors. "A thing? You're a psychic! You've solved over thirty crimes! You have something, dear! You're a super sleuth!"

"Simmer down, Isadora. I think the term super sleuth might be a stretch. I'm proud of the work I've done helping local law enforcement. I mean, maybe that is my thing. It just feels different than your roller derby thing."

"Oh, don't fret, dear. You're the champion of

happy marriages. That's a much better talent than being queen of divorce."

"Now you're talking." Grams and I share a chuckle.

Before we can start a second tape, Twiggy's perpetually inconvenienced voice echoes from the intercom speaker. "Willoughby's here. Should I send him up?"

Pressing the mother-of-pearl button on the left, I reply, "Yes, please, and thank you."

When the bookcase door slides open, I'm surprised Silas is already wearing spectacles. As I inspect his eyewear closer, they have rose-tinted lenses and thin brass arms that curve around his preternaturally large ears. Those are his alchemically enhanced glasses. The ones he uses when he wishes to see the ghost of my grandmother.

"Good morning, ladies." He nods at me and makes a fancy bow to Ghost-ma.

"What's that in—?"

My sentence hangs unfinished as Ghost-ma rushes toward the alchemist, attempting to snatch the item from his hand. As usual, she's gotten overly excited and lost her ability to manifest corporeal form.

Silas adjusts his brown bowtie and pulls the item closer as he waves off the ghost of Grams with a flick of his wrist. "I must ask you to maintain some degree of decorum, Isadora. I brought this helmet as a gift for your granddaughter."

"Oh! I see it now." Stepping forward, I point to the gift in my mentor's hand. "That's the helmet Grams wore when she played derby. Her name is even on there. Tipsy Kitty." As I lean closer, I see an additional word has been added more recently.

"Too? T-O-O." My blank stare demands assistance.

"I thought perhaps it would be an amusing bit of japery to play off your grandmother's name."

I have no idea what japery is, but I get the gist of what he's saying. "Yeah, I can be Tipsy Kitty Too. Works for me."

Grams has fallen unusually silent.

"Everything all right, Grams?"

"Some days, I miss being in an actual body, dear. Don't get me wrong. I'm extremely grateful to be here, in any form. The years I've come to spend with you have been some of the best in my life—afterlife. But—"

"You don't have to explain, Grams. Even though I've never been a ghost, I have talked to a few of them over the years. They all miss certain things about being alive. Hopefully, with a little help from Silas, I can do that helmet proud."

Silas trudges toward the scalloped-backed chair, which is always his seat of choice, and settles in with the helmet on his lap. He adjusts his fusty tweed coat, glances up at me, and narrows his gaze.

Clearly, I missed the memo. Quickly taking a seat on the sofa opposite his chair, I await further instruction.

"After we spoke, I prepared an alchemical working. I've placed sigils on the interior of this helmet, along with a proprietary tincture." The light reflects off the sheen on his bald pate. "As long as this helmet is strapped securely on your head, you will skate as well as, if not better than, the original Tipsy Kitty. If—"

"Grams! Did you hear that? Silas fixed me up with coordination. Heck, maybe I'll wear it all the time!"

Grams giggles until she ghost snorts and has to turn away to deal with a minor ectoplasm leak.

"It's not that funny, Grams. Never mind. I'll wear it for skating, and that's it."

"As I was saying." Mr. Willoughby's bushy eyebrows pinch together, and his tone indicates displeasure with my interruption.

"Apologies, Silas. Please continue."

"You may wear the helmet for a maximum of three hours per twenty-four-hour period. When you are not wearing the helmet, you should place it in a drawer or closet. The working requires darkness to recharge and replenish."

He holds the helmet up but does not hand it to me. "Do you understand the parameters of this working?"

"Yes. Three hours per day. Then keep it in the dark."

"Very well. As with any working, use caution and respect the power of the item you wield."

The moment suddenly feels overly cinematic, and my dark humor intervenes. Dropping to one knee, I bow as I accept the helmet. Visions of Harry Hamlin's Perseus in *Clash of the Titans* dance in my head.

"Do not make light of this exchange, Mizithra Achelois Moon."

Oops. Full, formal name territory. I have definitely pushed my luck.

"Thank you, Silas. This is a huge help. I know if I can get information from these skaters, we can figure out what happened."

"Will you be skating for the team associated with Broken Rock?"

I definitely don't want to admit that I hadn't given that bit of the undercover operation any thought. Might as well lean into my skill set of making things up as I go along. "I thought it would be better to skate for the home team. According to Boomer, there were only a few of the Slammer Jammers present at the gymnasium. I don't think they'd know much about what happened if they truly weren't involved."

"Excellent deductive reasoning. I shall leave this matter in your capable hands. Please keep me informed of your progress." Silas slowly rises to leave. A single thread hangs from the hem of his fusty coat and plays in the air, as a wily feline slinks out from under the large four-poster king-sized bed.

Golden eyes lock onto the motion.

With no indication that he has seen or heard the movement, Silas utters a single phrase. "Robin Pyewacket Goodfellow, I wish to disabuse you of this notion."

Pyewacket immediately pushes back onto his haunches, exposes his dangerous fangs in a disinterested yawn, and licks his left paw as though emerging for a bit of grooming was his intent all along.

Grams and I chuckle at the ever-present power struggle between the two wise creatures in our lives. Alchemist and caracal — or whatever is Pyewacket's true nature.

"Time to get down to the practice warehouse and see if they'll have me."

Silas shakes his head and silently ambles toward the door. "Call your Mr. Harper. He'll take you to obtain proper equipment for your venture." My mentor wanders out to the Rare Books Loft and begins mumbling to the tomes as though he's greeting old friends.

Grams swirls around in excitement. "Oh, sweetie. You must have an outfit!"

Blerg.

Time to call Erick and redeem my "Get out of Fashion-Jail Free" card.

Turns out I needed far more than a cute outfit. It takes almost an hour at Instant Replay, the used sporting goods store, to uncover all the gear I need to make the right impression when I show up at the warehouse for practice.

"Why do I need all this protective gear? Silas gave me the alchemical helmet thing-y. I'm gonna skate like a pro. No need to worry about falling over."

"It's not about falling over, Moon. You have no idea how rough it is out there. The other skaters are gonna be going just as hard as you. They'll be hitting you and knocking you off your feet. I don't care how magic that helmet is—"

Lifting my chin, I correct him. "*Alchemically*

enhanced." Silas would be so proud of me right now.

"Whatever you say. You need the equipment." Erick rifles through the items in the cart, saying them out loud as he crosses things off a mental checklist. "Kneepads, elbow pads, wrist guards, high-impact shorts, and skates."

"You're forgetting a couple things, Sheriff."

His big blue eyes look up at me, oozing hope and gratitude. "Knock it off. I haven't won yet."

"Hey, I'm with Johnson. Your winning the election is a foregone conclusion. I'm simply practicing early."

"Fine. What did I miss?"

"I think cute knee socks, a couple snarky T-shirts, and I probably need a belt or something, right?"

"Just wear one of the merch T-shirts you bought. It'll show them you support the team. I'm sure Isadora can take care of the rest of the wardrobe items."

My shoulders sag at the thought. "You're not wrong." I grab a cute pair of black knee socks with a skeleton pattern — just in case.

With that, we head to the register to complete our purchase.

"Wow. That's a ton of gear. Did you make the team?"

"What now?" I tilt my head and arch an eyebrow.

The woman behind the register tucks a strand of her poppy-red hair behind her ear and her lip piercing lifts as she grins. "You skate with the Rink Rashers, right?"

"Not yet. But soon."

"Oh. Good luck then."

The change in her tone feels like disappointment and a warning all wrapped together. Not sure whether it's my regular or my psychic senses filling in the blanks. I keep my concerns to myself. "Thanks. I think I've got a decent shot."

Her attention remains on the items as she rings them up, carefully avoiding any glances in my direction. "Yeah, totally. They're always looking for people to skate on the scrimmage team."

Yikes. She doesn't even know me, and she's already relegated me to the B team.

The clerk mumbles, "You wanna make a donation to the Boys and Girls Club to support after-school sports?" Her hand hovers above the register.

"Yeah, just add a hundred dollars to my bill."

Now, her youthful brown eyes lock onto my grey ones, and I relish the shock I observe.

"A hundred. Are you sure?"

"Absolutely. Big fan of the Boys and Girls Club."

She rings up the sale, and I hand her my cash. Because I always come prepared. Then my knight in well-worn blue jeans grabs all my bags.

As we push through the door, the bell dings and the clerk shouts an additional "good luck" in my wake.

"Let's head back to the bookstore so you can get kitted out. I'm sure Isadora has ten or fifteen options for you."

Chuckling, I hop into the car as he tosses everything in the trunk. Back at headquarters, my old apartment above the bookshop, Grams has indeed done a masterclass in wardrobe character study.

"So I'm not sure if they still wear the cute little skirts or just the shorty-short tap pants. So I have both options. And you look so good in red—"

"Grams! How many times do I have to tell you, the team colors are lime-green and black? I can't just roll up wearing whatever I want. If you don't have the colors, then I think I should stick to something neutral, like all black."

She giggles and bright anticipation floods her ethereal form. "You get too excited about being a Goth girl. Go handle your makeup, and I'll find something suitable."

"Makeup? Are you insane? I'm going to skate and sweat and hopefully pry some information out of these ladies. Why would I need makeup?"

Ghost-ma exhales and crosses her bejeweled limbs over her ample bosom. "Derby is all about brutal beauty, dear. At least put on some eyeliner. You've been living in luxury a bit too long. You've lost that hungry edge you had when you first came to town. You're not the same bad a—"

"Myrtle Isadora! Language!"

We giggle ourselves silly as I head into the bathroom next to the walk-in closet, which I generally refer to as *Sex and the City* meets *Confessions of a Shopaholic*, and dig through the drawers until I find a black eyeliner pen.

I'm no makeup genius, but I can throw down a dangerous cross between a smoky eye and a hungover Gena Gershon eye. Either way, I've got tough-gal eyeliner moves when necessary.

By the time I get back into the closet and plunk myself down on the padded mahogany bench, Grams has kept her word and assembled a lovely black outfit paired with the cute black and skeleton patterned knee socks I grabbed at Instant Replay — despite Erick's protest.

"I'm good with the outfit, but I need something to carry all this gear in, Grams."

"Check the storage closet by the children's book section, sweetie."

Returning to the hidden passage under the mezzanine provides a walk down memory lane. The wood has been scratched to kingdom come by the nasty little claws of Robin Pyewacket Goodfellow. When I took my first trip away from Pin Cherry, that secret sweetheart tried to hide in my luggage.

This hidden door still holds the title for the most difficult to open that I've encountered since the day I moved into the bookshop and started uncovering secret passages. My moody mood ring actually revealed the secret clue to twisting a small portrait hanging on the wall and depressing a button hidden beneath an embossed header strip of cloth wallpaper at the same time. If not for the ring's intermittent aid, I'm not sure I could've figured it out.

As I dig through the closet in search of a large duffle, Pyewacket waltzes in. "Hey, buddy. You worried I'm gonna ditch you?"

He skulks in the shadows and makes no response.

"What's up, son? You mad at me?"

Silence.

Turning to face the fiendish feline, I note the set of his jaw.

"Whatcha got there? It's not gonna explode on me, is it?" Reaching toward him, I pause for permission.

Pye blinks slowly, with an air of annoyance, before opening his jaws and dropping his prize.

"A gold crown-shaped lapel pin with a bent cross on the top?"

His wise golden gaze appraises me and finds me wanting.

"Understood. I'll add it to the murder board, even though I have zero idea how it ties in with our case."

"Ree-ow." Soft but condescending.

"Have patience, furry overlord. I'm merely human."

He makes a scoffing sound, steps forward, and grabs some black fabric with his teeth.

"Hey, that's exactly what I was looking for."

Pye drops the duffel bag and saunters out of the closet without a backward glance.

"Thank you, my liege."

"RE-ow." Feed me.

"I shall fill your goblet with Fruity Puffs before I pack this bag, your furriness."

Nothing. Not even a growl of gratitude. Such is the life of a caracal's servant.

Dragging the large empty duffel up the stairs is approximately forty-seven times easier than lugging it back down — filled with roller derby gear.

I'd love to text Erick for some help, but he left for the office, and it's best I learn how to haul this thing around for myself. After all, I wouldn't look very dangerous sashaying into the practice warehouse behind a Sherpa.

I place the large duffel in the back of my Jeep and drive toward a part of town I rarely visit. It's an industrial area not far from Final Destination and definitely off the beaten path. The one and only time I drove here on purpose was my first meeting with Artie, the snowplow driver. But that's another story.

Finally locating the warehouse, I park and march inside with my duffel bag. Eight or nine women are skating at a terrifying speed inside a duct-tape-marked track on the warehouse's cement floor. Four or five others are on the sidelines, in metal folding chairs, adjusting gear and shooting the breeze.

As I approach, the rapid banter in their native tongue, which I previously identified as Hungarian, comes to a sharp end.

"Who are you supposed to be?"

Assuming self-deprecation is the best way forward, I drop my bag, shrug, and reply, "I guess I'm fresh meat."

The girl called Lucky Harms gets to her feet, skates over, and offers a greeting. "Welcome. You must skate for a place."

"That's the plan." Oh, dear Silas, don't fail me now.

CHAPTER 12

GROWING UP IN FOSTER CARE had a lot of downsides, but, over the years, one thing transformed into an upside. The ability to be a near-instant mimic. Fitting in quickly as I bounced from one foster home to another became a way to blend in and avoid bullies. Of course, once I crossed paths with my foster brother Jarrell . . . I became the thing others wanted to avoid.

If only life gave us "do-overs."

A quick glance around the track gives me all the information I need.

Tossing my bag on the ground in front of the row of metal chairs, I sit down and put on my gear like a pro. Once my quad skates are tightened and my pads properly adjusted, I pull the special helmet from the bag and strap it on.

Cellblock Dee whips a hard right off the track and jump-skids to a stop in front of me. "Where you get that helmet?" Her accent turns the W into a V sound and the Th into a D.

My psychic tingles tell me she knows more about the helmet than me, so now is not the time to attempt a lie. "Belonged to my grandmother. She skated back in the day."

Dee gives the side of my helmet a friendly whack and nods. "We know this Tipsy Kitty. Her legend is on wall. She makes the first apex jump. Then it was just called 'jump.' You must know this." She wiggles her skates left and then right as she slowly backs away and sizes me up. "You a jammer?"

Again, honesty seems to be my best bet. "These hips are made for blocking."

A brief chuckle escapes before she calls to her coach. "Atlas! The fresh meat."

A man who looks like he stepped out of a time machine from the 1970s walks toward me with a broad smile and crinkling lines around his eyes. His huge "porn" stache is a reddish-brown, while his feathered hair leans more into the dishwater-blond territory.

"Hey there." He extends his hand and his leather blazer-style overcoat creaks. "Atlas Hahn. I own the team."

Trying not to chuckle at his huge lapel and flared bell bottoms, I grip his hand. "Hahn? Name sounds familiar. Do you run a business in town?"

His friendly grin widens. "Yeah. Wife and I own the Duds n' Suds Laundromat."

Snapping my fingers, I point to him. "That's it. I knew it sounded familiar. Great idea." I want to ask if it transforms into an after-hours disco, but Grams' voice echoes in my head. *You get more flies with honey.* "You've got a great team here."

He removes his mirrored sunglasses. "Good luck today."

Oddly sincere. "Thanks."

Atlas walks over to a skater with "Betty Beware" on her helmet and exchanges a few whispered instructions.

Hoping against hope that my helmet can compensate for all of my inborn disasters, I rise out of the chair with masked trepidation.

Following the movements of Cellblock Dee, I push off my right toe-stop and glide onto the track.

My first lap around is slow. I'm definitely checking out all the gear to make sure I know what I'm doing.

I feel weirdly confident.

On the next lap, I bend my knees and crouch into the skater's stance the other gals are taking. I'm picking up speed as I note a crossover motion they're doing with their feet when they round the corners of the oval track.

It feels natural. The speed is exhilarating.

This helmet is amazing!

Shoot! I forgot to check the time. Silas said only three hours a day. Announcing to no one that I need to tighten my skates, I return to the row of chairs and take a surreptitious peek at my phone.

11:03. All right. I gotta be out of this helmet no later than 2:03.

As I return to the track, Betty Beware blows the whistle and the official practice begins.

She glances my way. "Hey, fresh meat, try to keep up."

I nod and mentally cross my fingers.

The first drill is slow laps around the track. She blows the whistle. We squat for approximately thirty seconds as we keep rolling. Betty blows the whistle again. We stand and keep skating. By the third lap, my quads are on fire! The muscles in my thighs that is, not my skates.

Not sure how much more I can take, I'm pleased when the drill changes up. Now, we start on one side of the warehouse, skating straight through the track. When Betty Beware blows the whistle, we drop to our knees and slide. Getting up as quickly as possible.

I'm an absolute pro at falling. The getting up

part is not going as smooth as I'd hoped, but I'm holding my own.

Tweet. Tweet. Tweet. "Mona Madness. Cellblock Dee. Hold the stick."

The two skaters who were named grab a large push broom and unscrew the handle. They crouch on the track, holding it between them like a limbo pole, only much, much lower.

Cellblock Dee has a tattoo on her left thigh. A crown with a tilted cross on the peak. Pyewacket strikes again. But does it mean she's guilty? I wish that cat gave notes.

Betty Beware demonstrates the next move. She skates hard toward the broom handle and then jumps over it, in what I am guessing is this apex jump everyone's yammering on about.

Dear Lord baby Jesus! Come on, magic helmet.

We've formed a rough line, and, as each skater in front of me heads toward the broom handle, my heart beats faster and faster. Despite my mounting terror, I notice the crown with the tilted cross tattoo on three more skaters. Maybe it's a team thing. Like a championship symbol.

I guess Pyewacket meant for me to hang with this team.

Finally, I'm at the head of the line and it's my turn.

Making this jump could be the difference between earning a place on the team or not.

Skating fast, I push off my right foot, pull both knees up, and aim my skates for the track on the other side of the handle.

When I land, wobble, and skate away, I'm unable to prevent the raucous "Woot" that escapes my lips.

Betty Beware claps. "This is not bad for fresh meat. What are you doing Friday night?" Her accent is softer than Cellblock Dee's, but she still shifts the Th sound into a D.

"Hoping to skate with the Rink Rashers."

"Yes. You do this—" she points to the jump I recently made "—you skate with the team."

I'm in! I made the team! Erick and Grams are going to be so proud of me.

The practice continues with muscle-fatiguing drill after muscle-fatiguing drill. By the time we skate to the folding chairs to remove our gear, I'm absolutely whipped.

Betty and Dee, still in their full regalia, skate up to either side of me.

They exchange a few sentences in their native Hungarian, give each other a knowing nod, and turn toward me.

"You start blocking," says Betty Beware.

"Once you have strength, then you jam." Cellblock Dee gazes at me, appraising my "strength" and I see a flicker of admiration beneath her judgment.

"Sounds good. The next practice is Friday?"

Betty laughs so hard she has to bend over and support herself with a hand on each kneepad. "Next practice this afternoon. You skate in the bout this Friday. We play in Canada. Crooks Bay Rollers. Good? You have the passport?"

"I'm good." Did her gaze shift to Atlas when she said passport? "Definitely have a passport." I'm sure I have a passport — somewhere. I hope it's not expired. Glancing at my phone after removing my gear tells me I have one hour and fifteen minutes of helmet time left today. I hope the afternoon's practice is only an hour, or I'm going to be in deep trouble.

"Hey, did you guys hear about that accident at the high school? It happened Sunday night after your bout."

I'm careful to avoid looking eager. I'm simply loosening my skates and putting my gear back in the duffel bag. Making casual conversation.

Betty pushes back on her skates, and Cellblock Dee and Lucky Harms turn and skate to the track without a word. Glancing at the empty chairs beside me, and Betty's frightened face, I attempt to use some of my so-called humor.

"I guess I better change my deodorant. Cleared the place right out." The hollow ring of my false laughter does nothing to alter the expression on Betty's face. Her pupils are dilated, and her body language screams fear loud enough for even the mundane to hear.

Unfortunately, the exhaustion is fiddling with my psychic perceptions. I'm not getting any clear information about who or what she fears. She knows something. Maybe I can invite—

Cellblock Dee calls Betty to the track as I pack up the rest of my gear. So much for winning friends and influencing people to spill their guts on day one. Here's to having better luck in Crooks Bay. Yeesh, I hope that town's name is some kind of hilarious pun . . .

Walking back to my Jeep is an exercise in the ridiculous. After an hour and forty-five minutes of wearing heavy quad skates that make me four inches taller, my equilibrium is wonky.

My legs feel like jelly, and I'm not entirely sure I have the strength left in my feet to press the gas pedal, let alone slam on the brakes in case of emergency.

Maybe I should have worried less about skating and more about recovery. I'll have to rifle through that hidden drawer of supplies in my old apartment and see if I have one of those handy little recovery tinctures from the secret pockets of Silas Willoughby's tattered tweed coat.

Here's hoping.

CHAPTER 13

A QUICK TEXT to Erick confirms he's still in the office. Rather than heading back to Bell, Book & Candle, I drive straight to Harper and Moon Investigations.

Unsurprisingly, my husband is alone in the office. It's not the kind of place that gets a ton of walk-in traffic.

The handsome, soon-to-be sheriff looks up with a smirk. "Hey, I like your outfit."

Offering him a complimentary shake of my tail feathers, I chuckle and collapse onto the small sofa. "That helmet works a treat. But we've got another practice this afternoon, and I'm beat."

Erick rises from his chair, tosses his pen on the partners desk he pretends to share with me, and walks in my direction with a subtle grin lifting his cheeks. "Is that something your mom used to say?"

"Which thing?"

"'Works a treat.' I don't have much experience, but it seems like a British phrase." He squeezes onto the couch next to me and kisses my cheek.

A wave of emotion washes over me and my heart aches. It's been over a decade since I lost my mom, yet all the feels can still hit me out of nowhere. "Yeah, I guess it is. There's so little of her remaining, but at least there are some tiny pieces. Even if I don't consciously realize it."

He wipes a sweaty strand of hair from my face as he nods. "Yeah, I keep telling myself that my mom is invincible, but I'm going to have to face it sooner or later. Her macular degeneration gets worse every year, but Gracie stays strong and always sounds positive. She loves living with her sister in Florida, but her last letter was filled with several not-so-subtle hints." Erick chuckles and leans his head back against the wall.

Laying my sweaty head on his shoulder, I offer support. "Let's get her a ticket. It's been a few months since her last visit. She's easy to have around, and despite her visual impairment, she cooks about a thousand percent better than me!"

A sigh of contentment slowly drifts from Erick.

"Have I mentioned that your nomination for world's best wife was sent in last week?"

Punching him playfully on the shoulder, I counter, "Well, I guess I better get busy on your world's best husband nomination. How embarrassing would it be to stand up there alone?"

Joking about this imaginary awards banquet is a warm touchstone in our young relationship. I hope we're still able to banter like this in fifty years.

Wow. Fifty years! Seems like an eternity. My grandmother mowed through five husbands in half that time. Part of me may always wonder what else is out there, but it's such a tiny part that I don't bother to give it the time of day. I found the perfect match. He accepts me — warts and all. Somehow I'm becoming the best version of myself, simply by having him in my life.

"Where'd you go, Moon?"

"It's probably best if I don't tell you. Let's just all agree that I wandered off into one of my mind movies and didn't hear a thing you were saying."

"I'm gonna call my mom and see when she wants to fly out. You sure about this?" Erick pulls out his phone as he leans forward.

"Of course. Call Gracie. Make it happen. I need to get home, shower, and nap before the next practice."

"What about food? A girl can't skate two-a-dayers on an empty stomach."

"Two-a-dayers?"

"Yeah, that's what we called 'em back when I played high-school football. It was brutal. At least you're indoors and not out in the baking-hot summer sun."

"Summer? I thought high-school football started in the fall?"

He lifts one eyebrow and shrugs. "Officially? You'd be correct. However, everybody knew that if they wanted any chance of making the starting lineup, they had to show up for summer practice. Coach never made it mandatory. But we all knew." He gets to his feet and rakes his fingers through his slicked-back blond hair. "We all knew."

As I attempt to hop up and kiss him goodbye, my legs give out and I find myself right back where I started. Erick chuckles. "May I help you out to your car, m'lady?"

"You might have to help me all the way home. I'm not sure I'll be able to stand up in the shower." When I utter my comment, I mean it in the most innocent of ways.

As Erick grabs my hand, pulls me to my feet, and firmly to his chest, the heat in his eyes indicates he's developed an interpretation all his own.

"Is that an invitation?"

"Oh brother. I love you, Harper, but I do not have the energy."

"Fair enough. I'll give you twenty minutes, and then I'll swing by to pick you up for lunch. Sound good?"

"Sounds divine."

CUT TO—

Erick and I seated in our favorite corner booth, and the sound of french fries sizzling in hot oil.

"I got absolutely nowhere with my attempts to pry information out of the other skaters. Maybe I'll have more luck on the ride to Crooks Bay."

Erick chokes on his iced tea, wipes his mouth with the thin paper napkin, and swallows with difficulty. "The ride to where?"

"I think it's in Canada." My thoughts drift to the passport question. "Oh, I was so exhausted I forgot to tell you the good news. I made the team! Plus, they asked me to skate in their bout against the Crooks Bay Rollers Friday night."

"Mitzy, we have no idea who you're dealing with. One of those girls could be a murderer."

"I think we're calling them women now." I flash a smug lip shrug. "What better way for me to see if there's any damage to their van than to take a little ride?"

My hubby is not amused with my rationale.

"I'm calling CC. I wanna make sure he's at the bout."

The mention of Erick's Army buddy, a suave French-Canadian, who's now a Canadian Mountie, brings a wicked smirk to my face.

Erick tilts his head. "Hey, I don't like that look. Let's all remember CC is happily married."

"What are you getting at? Let's all remember, *I'm* happily married. Aren't I?"

His reply is interrupted by the approach of Odell.

"Hey, Gramps. I'm so hungry I could—"

Odell sets the plate down, and I immediately notice the double-high pile of fries.

"What's that you were saying, kid?" His dark-brown eyes twinkle as he places meatloaf and mashed potatoes in front of my husband.

Yep, I definitely inherited some of my abilities from good old Gramps.

"Love that T-shirt." Odell shakes his head and chuckles as he raps his knuckles twice on the table before heading back to his domain.

Today's post-practice tee features the all-too-appropriate phrase, "Keep your eyes on the fries" below a bountiful basket of french fries.

After two enormous bites of my burger, a couple handfuls of fries, and a long slurp of my soda, my growling stomach takes a backseat.

"Hey, my dad's calling. I should take it."

Erick, too polite to speak with his mouth full, simply nods in agreement.

"Hey, Dad, I thought you and Amaryllis were somewhere on the East Coast handling new agreements for the rail yard. Everything all right?"

Turns out my dad had a very unexpected reason for calling.

"What? Are you sure? No, I thought it was a coincidence. Nobody had any connection. Thanks, Dad. No. Seriously. Super helpful lead. Love you." Before I can slip my phone back into my pocket—

"What's up with your dad? Sounded important." Erick stops eating, and his posture is all business.

"It was. He got a call from the harbormaster. Turns out there was a connection between the victim and some unsavory dealings."

"That kid, Jason Samson, was involved in something illegal?" Erick leans toward me.

"No. His father. Ken Samson. I think it was Twiggy who told me about Jason's dad hurting his back in an accident on the docks. I didn't pay much attention. But the harbormaster said Ken was implicated in smuggling, narcotics trafficking, and there were even rumors of human trafficking before his mysterious back injury took him away from the docks."

Erick laces his fingers together behind his head and leans back.

You guessed it. My gaze darts downward, hoping to catch a peek of those washboard abs. That's right, we've been married two years, and my adorable husband is still keeping it all together for me.

"Good lead. I better call Boomer and see what he can pull up on this Ken Samson. If Ken was involved in that many illegal scams, there's got to be something on his sheet."

"You mean rap sheet?"

"Yeah, his rap sheet, Kojak."

His old-school dig makes me laugh. "I gotta devour this food and get a quick nap before practice. Avert your gaze, Harper."

Erick shakes his head. I dig in, and I won't apologize for it.

CHAPTER 14
ERICK

WHILE MITZY GETS SQUARED AWAY for her afternoon practice, I need to follow up with Ken Samson before the lead goes cold.

As I back the Nova out of the garage, my thoughts drift to memories of sitting behind the wheel of the sheriff's cruiser. I loved that feeling. Protecting the community. Serving the people of Pin Cherry Harbor and Birch County. I was being completely honest when I told Mitzy that I enjoy the work we do together at the investigations agency, but it's not the same.

Maybe I'm imagining the connection, but I've always felt better when I've had a sense of duty. I had a purpose when I was on call twenty-four hours a day and never shied away from putting in overtime for zero compensation. It wasn't for the money. It was always for the people.

Geez. I'm wandering off inside my own head like Mitzy.

Pushing away plans of returning to the sheriff's department, I focus on coming up with a strategy as I head out to the Samson place. Ken must've run most of his dirty deals in Broken Rock. I only remember dragging him in for drunk and disorderly and driving while intoxicated. Sounds like Boomer and the squad over in the Rock had more serious run-ins.

Mr. Samson is probably not going to want to talk to law enforcement. I definitely need to wear my civilian hat as I approach this one. Maybe I should get Mitzy? She definitely has a way about her. Not just her special abilities, or whatever. She seems to know how to put people at ease and get them talking. Or pummel them with questions until they crack.

Nah. I can do this. I used to interrogate folks for a living. Had a pretty good record, if I do say so myself.

Maybe it's time to get in touch with my inner sheriff, disguised as plain old Erick Harper.

The Samsons live in a part of town most Pinners try to forget. The tattered sign reads Rainbow's

End. But what lies beyond it is far from a pot of gold.

Row upon row of broken-down, ramshackle single-wide trailers — most of them poorly insulated — providing little shelter from the brutal winters this far north.

People tend to wind up here after they've fallen on hard times. Although, if memory serves, the Samsons have always lived out here.

Maybe there was a time when Rainbow's End was well-maintained and attractive, but that was long before I ever visited the place.

Back in high school, one of my best friends lived in the End. I used to hop off the bus here and do homework or watch TV until my mom picked me up. Looking back, it was free babysitting for her. I'm sure she imagined I'd get into less trouble hanging out with a buddy than I would on my own.

Unfortunately, she couldn't have been further from the truth.

Me and Westie knew how to get into the kind of trouble only young boys can find. Shoplifted firecrackers. Hiked to the dump and collected materials to build an unpermitted treehouse deep in the forest. And I had my first taste of moonshine at Westie's. His dad ran a little homebrew operation and stored a jug under the kitchen sink.

The memory of that taste still makes my stomach twist with nausea and shudder in protest.

There's a beat-up pickup truck parked next to the Samson's trailer. Parking my car behind the truck, I take a deep breath, remind myself I'm a civilian on a fact-finding mission, and head for the storm door, which is hanging by the top hinge.

Their front steps are stacked cinderblocks. No mortar, just blocks.

Perching precariously on top of the stack, I avoid the rickety outer door and knock directly on the doorjamb.

A woman with big pink curlers in her hair and a cigarette hanging from the corner of her mouth, yanks open the door with a grunt. "Not interested." Before she closes the door, I have to sputter out something.

"I need to talk to Ken."

The cigarette dangling from her chapped lips drops a chunk of ash onto the threadbare carpet.

"Ken! Some idiot here wants to talk to you." She turns and leaves the interior door ajar, but doesn't actually invite me in.

Since I'm not representing any law enforcement agency, I don't need permission or a warrant. Easing the battered screen door open, I step inside and take shallow breaths.

The apartment reeks of cigarette smoke, mold, and decay.

Ken stumbles out of the back in a sleeveless undershirt and thinning boxers held together by sheer luck.

Swallowing hard, I hope that luck doesn't run out. "Are you Ken Samson?"

He rubs his ruddy cheeks as bleary eyes attempt to focus in my direction. When he finally hones in on me, his demeanor snaps to attention.

You'd imagine he's suddenly wearing a three-piece suit as he attempts to square his shoulders and stand up straight.

"Hey, Sheriff. What can I do ya for?"

"Hey, Ken. I'm not here on official business." No need to remind him I'm no longer the sheriff. Let him think what he will. I never said it. Huh, looks like I did learn a thing or two from Mitzy. "Mind if I sit down?"

As soon as the words have been spoken, I catch sight of the stained sofa and wish I hadn't asked.

"Sure. Make yourself at home, Sheriff." Ken wanders over in his state of undress and shouts to his wife, "Tammy, why dontcha serve some refreshments?" Tammy's scratchy voice replies from the depths of the trailer. "Get 'em yourself."

Waving away his attempt at hospitality, I continue. "I'm fine, Ken. I wanted to stop by and tell you how sorry I was to hear about your boy."

Ken exhales forcefully, and the stench of stale booze engulfs me. His face cartwheels through a montage of emotions before sticking the landing on anger.

"If I find out who done it, I don't have to tell you, I'll take matters into my own hands."

"It's probably best if you don't say anything else along that line, Mr. Samson."

His watery eyes swim across my face, then he sniffs sharply. "'Course, that's just talk."

"Of course. I know you want this person brought to justice as much as I do. Part of the reason I stopped by, Ken, was to see if you had any information for me. You had more than your share of run-ins with some unsavory individuals, and I thought maybe this could be some kind of retaliation. Did you upset anybody enough to draw this kind of fire?"

"Me?" Ken attempts to straighten up his hungover, or possibly still drunk, posture and forces a look of sincerity onto his face. "I never made nobody that angry. Who does that? Who snuffs out a kid in his prime?" Ken's voice catches in his throat. Despite his state of inebriation, the pain of losing a son cuts through the fog.

"That's what I intend to find out, Mr. Samson.

If you could give me any information about anyone you might've crossed in the past, it would be immensely helpful. We just have nothing to go on right now."

His face scrunches, and he scrapes his fingers across his stubble. "I thought they arrested that skater girl from Broken Rock?"

"They did, but they don't have much in the way of evidence. Looks like the damage to the van may have been caused by a previous accident."

"I mighta—"

A harsh voice calls from the back of the trailer, "Shut your mouth, Ken."

Ken's meaty fist pounds on the cracked vinyl of his recliner. "I know I done some bad stuff, Sheriff. Ever since I messed up my back, I've been keeping my nose clean. Ya know what I mean?"

"I hope so. What about before you hurt your back? Any of those folks still running?" My attempt to keep the term vague is simply a tactic to draw out names of anyone doing anything that he's willing to share.

"Nah. There's new players in town. The kinda stuff that's way outta my league."

Muscles in my shoulders tense as I lean forward. "Like what?"

"Oh, I don't know. Ya hear stuff. Who knows what's true anymore?"

Ken's eyelids sag. I fear he'll be back sleeping one off before I can get anything useful.

"Do you mind if I have a look at Jason's room?"

Deep, resonant snoring is my only reply.

Getting to my feet, I shuffle past the overflowing trash bin in the kitchen and call out to Mrs. Samson. "Tammy, mind if I have a look at Jason's room? It might help the investigation."

She grunts something that I choose to interpret as permission, and I head down the narrow hallway.

The first door on the right appears to be a young man's bedroom.

A stained futon pushed into the corner, and a game controller partially buried under cast-off clothes.

There are half-empty dirty dishes littering nearly every flat surface, and I'm about to give up when I catch sight of something peeking out from under his rumpled blanket.

Navigating through the minefields littering the floor, I reach out and pull the covers back.

A phone? A phone! I have no idea why a young guy leaves his house without his phone, but I need to take that into evidence.

Shoot! I'm not the sheriff. I don't take things into evidence. Suddenly, I can almost hear Mitzy whispering in my ear.

You may as well collect it before it gets lost. I'm

sure Sheriff Paulsen would appreciate you turning it in.

A soft chuckle vibrates my chest. "Tammy, can you bring me a plastic sandwich bag?"

The sound of Tammy's inconvenienced footfalls grows closer. "Whaddya need a bag for?"

"With your permission, I'd like to take Jason's phone into evidence. Might help us figure out who took your son's life."

Tammy's eyes are bloodshot and red-rimmed. It's only now that I notice she looks as though she's been crying for days.

"Mrs. Samson, I'm sorry for your loss. There could be information on this phone that will help us catch Jason's killer."

She pulls a pack of cigarettes from the pocket of her housecoat and lights a fresh one. "I'll get you a bag."

Tammy disappears, returns, and hands me the bag. "It's locked, you know. We don't know his passcode. He didn't trust us." She flicks ash on one of the filthy plates on the dresser and watches closely as I recover the cell phone.

Turning the bag inside out, I reach for the phone, carefully enveloping it in the bag. Once it's bagged, I slip it into the pocket of my jacket.

"Thank you, Mrs. Samson. I'll see myself out."

That first hit of clean air is like a drug. My lungs tingle with joy at the burst of fresh oxygen.

I can't wait to tell Mitzy the good news. I'll have to take the phone into Paulsen as soon as possible, but not before Mitzy takes a crack at figuring out that passcode. It won't hurt anything for us to have a quick peek.

CHAPTER 15

SUDDENLY, I'm bolt upright in bed and beads of cold sweat paste my snow-white hair to my temples. My hands are shaking. My heart is racing. Steadying my finger to press the speed dial for *Secret Alchemist* seems a monumental task. I hit speaker and fall back against my pillow.

Mr. Willoughby answers on the first ring, and I plow ahead. "Silas, I had an absolute bonkers dream just now. I need to know what it means."

"Good afternoon, Mizithra. I trust you are well?" Kudos to his ability to avoid answering the question and somehow simultaneously teach me a lesson.

"I don't have time for manners. It was a dream about my mother. And a powerful magical — maybe alchemical — object."

His demeanor changes in an instant. "Are you quite certain it was a dream? It may have been a communication with your mother's spirit. Has Coraline Moon previously spoken to you in this manner?"

It's not often I find myself at a loss for words. The thought that naptime's strange vision could be more than the wishful thinking of a girl orphaned at eleven nearly stops my heart. "Not like this. This time, I felt her in her physical form. She hugged me. Then she gave me the strangest message."

Silas harrumphs, and a long, slow exhale swallows up nearly a minute before he replies.

"We are learning more about your abilities with each passing day. What you have described could be astral travel. An out-of-body experience. Based on my interpretations of the arcane and my knowledge of the spirit world, I believe this to have been a visitation. Not merely a phantasm of dreamland. Do you recall the message?"

"I'll never forget it as long as I live." The hairs on the back of my neck stand on end.

My mentor's tone is calm but stern. "Tell me. You must repeat it verbatim. Each syllable spoken by the energies on the other side of the veil carries an import our minds can scarcely comprehend. Take a deep breath, sink into the memory, and recite exactly what Coraline said to you."

Disappearing into the precious memory of my mother's touch is easy. I never want to leave this place. As her arms loosen and her hands slide downward, she grips my fingers in hers. Gentle dark eyes seem to stare through mine — to my soul. Her beautiful British voice fills my head.

"My sweet girl, I have learned of a powerful relic. On this side of the veil, it is known as the Oracle of Return. Find it. Speak my name into its ear. I shall return to you. Whole. Unblemished. As though I never left."

A hollow, empty silence hangs over the phone line. Eventually, I fear the call may have been disconnected.

"Silas? Are you there?" A sharp inhale is his only response.

"What does it mean?" My heart feels as though it could beat out of my chest.

"You are certain those were her exact words. The Oracle of Return?"

"Yes. I'm one thousand percent sure. I'm using my psychic recall. Why? What is it?"

His voice is soft, almost awestruck. "I have existed my entire life believing it to be a myth. I thought surely if anyone could learn of its existence, it would be your grandmother. When Isadora left this physical realm and made no report of such an object, I felt the matter was closed and ended my inquiries. But—"

My tendency to blurt intervenes. "But Grams never crossed over! You said yourself that her experiences are different from spirits who exist on the other side of the veil. She's — tethered."

"Indeed, you are most wise. Did your mother tell you of the Oracle's purpose?"

"No. Some loud noise in the house abruptly pulled me from the dream — or whatever it was. I didn't even have a chance to say goodbye." My voice catches in my throat as tears threaten.

Another lingering silence tests my patience. "I must recover my research from the vault. I will call you within the hour."

"Wait! You have to tell me something. What does it mean? What's the Oracle?"

"The Oracle of Return, on this side of the veil, has long been known as 'az Út a világok között.' The Way between the Worlds."

"Like an actual way back from death? Like I could bring my mother back? Back to the physical plane to live with me?" I want to continue asking questions, but a sob rips from my throat, and heavy tears sluice down my cheeks.

"Yes." His tone is soft, but steady.

When a man who prides himself on offering the most complex and convoluted responses replies with a single word — it feels as though the earth has stopped turning.

"We have to find it. Whatever you need me to do, any help I can offer with my abilities — we have to find it."

He harrumphs. I picture him smoothing his bushy mustache and adjusting his tattered tweed coat. "Objects of power are well hidden, for obvious reasons, Mizithra. The Oracle of Return contains immense power. Such an artifact can only be used once. All of the energy imbued would be consumed when it is activated." A long sigh leaks over the phone. "It may no longer exist. Perhaps its use triggered the resurfacing of the legend. I shall call you the minute I have news." Silas ends the conversation without so much as a farewell.

His strange actions continue to impress upon me the veracity and weight of my mother's message.

A single use. One chance to be reunited.

My heart wants to latch onto it, but my head refuses to let hope bloom.

If I were serious about napping, I would stay in the three-story walk-up, where I'm protected from ghost-trusions by wards and sigils. It's not free from intrusions of the tan terror, but I don't think there's any place on earth that's truly Pyewacket-proof.

The initial exhaustion of the roller derby practice has faded. The strange dream has me pumped with fresh energy.

I'm excited to share my news with Ghost-ma. The roller derby news, that is. I'll hold off on any mention of the strange message from my late mother until Silas comes up with something concrete.

Making my way across the bookshop, through the Rare Books Loft, and into my old apartment, I'm unsurprised to find Pyewacket stretched across the pillow-y down comforter atop the antique four-poster bed, clearly displaying his ownership of any space he occupies.

"Hey, where's Grams?"

"REE-ow!" A warning.

"Don't take that tone with me, son. I know quite a few of your secrets."

The mention of secrets brings a quick twitch of his black-tufted ears, but no further information.

"Grams?" Once more, with feeling. "Grams!"

A swoosh of ethereal vapor fires out of the walk-in closet. "Oh no! What did you break?"

"Rude. I can't believe you assumed I failed."

She avoids additional commentary, but she offers no apology.

"I didn't crash, but the day wasn't a total success."

"Oh, sweetie, it's tough to make the team. We'll

come up with some other way for you to get information from those gals."

Yeesh. "Isadora, I'm gonna need a little more positivity from you. For your information, I skated like a champ. I absolutely made the team. They even invited me to skate in the away game this Friday night in Crooks Bay."

Grams claps her hands and circles around me like a puppy with the zoomies.

"You're gonna need to simmer down. It's not all good news." I struggle to keep some of my thoughts private.

She furrows her shimmering brow and spins one of her many bejeweled rings. "It never is, dear. Now, what are you trying to hide from me?"

"Grams!" I point to my closed lips. "Absolutely no thought-dropping!" With an enormous put-upon exhale, I flop onto the sofa. "The skaters were all pretty tightlipped. The owner was friendly, but the girls on the team keep to themselves. A couple of them talked to me, but not more than a few words."

She taps a perfectly manicured finger on her coral lip. "Who owns the team?"

"Some guy named Atlas Hahn. Same guy who owns the launderette."

"Launderette? What are you saying, sweetie?"

"Weird. I did it again. Something my mother

always said. I meant to say laundromat. It just came out wrong."

Grams hovers directly in front of me, and her glowing hand gently strokes my cheek. "It didn't come out wrong at all. If that was something Coraline Moon used to say, then it's the most right thing ever. You go ahead and call it a launderette. And I'll haunt anyone who says different."

Without thinking it through, I throw my arms around Grams, and they fold in upon themselves and land limp at my sides. "I tried. I know you can't feel it, Grams, but I'm hugging you in my mind."

Her ghostly eyes fill with tears. "But I can feel it, sweetie. I feel it every time. I get this tingle in my energy, and I know someone who loves me is thinking about me. It's magnificent. It took me a couple of years as a ghost to figure out what was going on, but now that I know — it's a bit like a drug."

"Easy. We both know your tendency toward addiction. I'm not sure they have an afterlife chapter of AA, but I think you should be happy with whatever happens and not use words like drug or addicted."

Ghost-ma's expression turns serious, and she presses a hand to her chest. "You're so right, dear. I appreciate you pointing that out. Anyhoo, the feeling is a lovely gift whenever it happens. I don't expect it, and I don't need it. Hashtag Blessed."

We both laugh until happy tears spill forth.

"Did I use it right?" She seems genuinely concerned.

Nodding my head and holding my stomach as I attempt to get my laughter under control, I reply, "Totally. You're the hippest ghost I know."

Grams tugs at the edges of her Marchesa gown and gives me a comical curtsy. "I do my best."

"And I need to do my best. I've got one more practice today and then the game on Friday. As much as these gals skate, they probably have a practice in the morning even though they have a game tomorrow night!"

She floats aimlessly toward the bank of 6 x 6 windows overlooking the great lake. "Time and distance are hard concepts to hold onto in this in-between place, but if memory serves, it's a two-hour drive to Crooks Bay. I can't imagine them having a practice tomorrow. You better get back over to the rink."

Pushing myself to a sitting position, I stretch my arms and chuckle. "Rink is a generous term. They've got some duct tape on the cement floor of a warehouse. Not exactly a rink."

Grams seems to transform into a schoolmarm as she admonishes me for my judgment. "Not everyone is lucky enough to be an heiress, young lady. Maybe you should count your blessings as you drive over to practice."

"You're not wrong, Grams." Pressing the plaster medallion embossed with vines of twisted ivy that opens the secret door, I toss one over my shoulder. "Hashtag Blessed."

She giggles.

"Oh, and if you can roll out the corkboard and add the empty food coloring bottle and that lapel pin to the murder board . . ."

Her ghostly salute disappears behind the sliding bookcase as I exit.

With that, I head back to the walk-up, load my gear in the Jeep, and drive straight to the PI office. I expected an update from Erick some time ago.

His vehicle isn't parked outside the office, but I pull into the lot anyway. Grabbing my phone, I fire off a text. "What gives, Harper?"

If only I had the ability to force people to reply to my text messages in a timely manner.

Placing both hands on the phone, I squeeze my eyelids tight and chant. "Text me. Text me. Text me."

PING.

The incoming text notification shocks me, and I drop the phone in my lap.

No way! It worked.

"Meeting with some old CIs. I'll grab dinner from Angelo and Vinci's and catch you up after your practice."

That's definitely not the information I was hoping for. Maybe my terse reply will let him know he's falling down on the job.

"10-4."

Before I drop my phone into the cup holder, a laughing emoji pops up on the screen.

See, he gets me.

Time to get back in the rink.

Pulling out of Harper and Moon Investigations, I drive to the warehouse.

My second practice of the day is going far better than expected. However, it's also going longer than expected. One minute, I'm sailing around the track, hip-checking the skaters playing as the opposing team in a scrimmage, and the next, I'm sprawled across the cement slowly sliding headfirst toward the folding chairs.

Chants of "Fall small!" echo in my wake. Whatever that means.

Cellblock Dee skates over and helps me to a seat on one of the chairs. "What happened? Is this some dirt on the track?"

Having no idea what dirt on the track would have to do with the sudden malfunction in my helmet, I grab onto it like a life preserver in an angry sea. "Must've been. I think I need a minute."

She shakes her head. "You're done now. We need your best tomorrow night. You rest."

"Yes, ma'am. Whatever you say."

Dee grabs my bag and kicks it toward my feet. I peel off my gear, stuff it in the duffel, and ask what time practice starts in the morning.

Betty Beware laughs lightly and juts her chin at Cellblock Dee. "She's a good pick."

My eyes dart back and forth between the two team leaders. Cellblock Dee looks toward Atlas, and he saunters over. "Nope. No practice tomorrow, Tipsy. We leave at noon. I'm working on getting a vehicle big enough to hold the team."

"Don't you have a team van?"

His gaze narrows, but his voice remains friendly. "Something's wrong with the engine. I'm getting the plugs changed and I asked them to put in a new fuel filter. They'll take care of it, but it won't be ready by tomorrow."

This could be my ticket to the inner circle. I need to be a hero. "I might be able to get you a school bus. I'm good friends with the snowplow driver. She's got an 'in' over at the bus barn. Want me to check it out?"

Atlas pushes the edge of his ridiculous mustache between his teeth and chews on it while he has a think. "When will you know?"

"Um, probably not till first thing tomorrow morning, but maybe tonight. I can call Dee—"

He jumps in before I can finish my sentence. "No need. Call me directly."

"All right. Sure."

Grabbing the sharpie from my duffel, I ask for his number and write it on my arm. Something deep within my extrasensory perception tells me not to get out my phone.

"Great practice, everybody. I'll let you know about the bus as soon as I hear. Thanks again for letting me join the team."

Several of the girls wave. Atlas continues to snack on the edge of his 'stache.

Ewww, and weird. Never had a mustache, so I have no idea if that's a thing. Time to call Erick and see if he can swing another favor from Artie, even though he doesn't have the power of the badge behind him this time.

Not yet, anyway.

CHAPTER 16

ARRIVING HOME to the delicious aroma of Angelo and Vinci's irresistible lasagna is exactly what I need after my intense day of skating.

My inner film-school dropout can't resist making an entrance. As I push through the door marked *Employees Only* leading from the bookshop into the walk-up, I call out, "Honey, I'm home."

To my delight, Detective-Too-Hot-To-Handle is shirtless in the kitchen, putting plates and flatware on the table.

No matter how many times I'm blessed with this vision, those abs always stop me in my tracks.

"What's the matter, Moon? Cat got your tongue?"

Pyewacket utters a sound that too closely mimics a snicker.

"First of all, I don't appreciate it when you two gang up on me, and B, can we get a shirt on this guy?" My *Date Night* callback is solely for my private amusement.

Erick laughs and motions for me to join him at the table. "The weather was so gorgeous today, I couldn't resist taking a run. I just got out of the shower, but can't seem to cool down."

Swallowing with difficulty, I approach the table. "You're telling me."

"Sorry, I missed that." He closes the distance between us, and, despite my post-practice sweat, he wraps his arms around me and kisses me softly.

"Nice try, Harper. Unfortunately, my stomach pretty much always defeats my heart in battle. I gotta eat something."

Hanging his head in mock sorrow, he pulls out my chair like the gentleman he always is.

"Tell me about your day, Hubby. Did you turn up anything helpful?"

He lifts the corner of his placemat to reveal his surprise. Erick pulls out a baggie and slides it toward me. My shoulders shrug of their own accord. "What am I looking at?"

He leans back and sniffs sharply. "You're the psychic. You tell me."

"Touché."

As I reach toward the plastic sandwich bag, the

band on my left ring finger turns into a circlet of ice. Glancing into the smoky-black cabochon, I see the face of a young man in his prime. The name *Jason* swirls around my head like a kite lost in a storm.

"Did you get a hold of Jason Samson's phone?"

His smug grin belies the guilt in his sweet blue-grey eyes.

"Erick No Middle Name Harper! Did you re-move evidence from a crime scene? I had no idea how much I was rubbing off on you." Now it's my turn to look smug.

"Don't get ahead of yourself. It wasn't an official crime scene, and Tammy Samson gave it to me. Plus, I fully intend to turn the phone over to Paulsen." He shifts in his chair, discomfort rolling off him in waves.

Pressing two fingers to my temple, I put on an extrasensory perception pantomime. "Wait. I'm get-ting something. You want me to crack the code and do a little super snooping before you hand it off to Paulsen." Gazing at him from the corner of my eye, I add, "How am I doing?"

The guilt floods over him, and he swallows with difficulty. "Could you?"

Flipping the phone over — without removing it from the plastic — I awaken it and take a deep, cleansing breath.

You guessed it, every time I take a deep,

cleansing breath, I can't help but think how much airy-fairy woo-woo nonsense I ignored working as a broke-as-Little-Women barista back in Sedona. Turns out that stuff was way truer than I imagined.

Numbers sound off in my head like the sharp call of a drill sergeant to his troops. My thumb seems to move with a mind of its own.

"I'm in."

Erick leans forward and whispers, "I didn't doubt you for a second."

The hair on my arms stands on end, and I can almost imagine what it must be like for people who can't communicate with ghosts. Whenever Grams brushes against most mortals, they get chill bumps up and down their arms. I've never experienced it, but this is close.

Tapping the icon for messages, Erick and I hold our breath in unison.

There it is. The last message Jason Samson ever received.

"Meet behind the gym. Don't bring your phone. They're tracking you."

A wave of emotion hits me. I drop the baggie and its contents on the table as I draw a ragged breath. "Who would do this? They lured him to his death, Erick."

A strong hand rubs my back as he chews the inside of his cheek. He's giving off vibes of sorrow and anger in equal measure.

"Can you use your law enforcement contacts to track this number? Whoever sent this text is the murderer. Case closed."

He leans back and pushes his plate away. "Ten to one it's a burner phone. People who plan murders aren't usually geniuses, but something tells me this one is smarter than average."

"Why? Because he knew Jason was being tracked? Who would have been tracking a college kid?"

Erick shakes his head. "You really must be exhausted. Usually, you're one step ahead of me. There was no one tracking Jason. The killer simply didn't want this phone on Jason's person. He would've had to touch it to erase this text message after the murder. Telling the kid to leave his phone at home meant no evidence at the scene. Kept the killer's identity hidden or at least bought him enough time to get out of town."

I exhale in defeat. A lot of people can't eat when they get upset. I've only had that problem once. And today is not that day.

Grabbing my fork, I dig into the lasagna and let the warm, spicy tomato sauce and gooey melted cheese soothe my spirit.

Erick reluctantly follows suit, and a heavy silence hangs between us.

As usual, I finish first. Then I gulp half my glass of Chianti and swipe at a dribble of wine with the back of my hand.

"Were you able to get anything from the dad? Any information about the deals he got into when he worked at the docks? What about the CIs you were talking to? Did they know anything about the va—"

Before Erick has a chance to answer even one of my questions, I smack the heel of my hand into my forehead. "I totally forgot! The team needs a bus. When I asked Atlas what happened to the team van, he got all bajiggity. I mean, he covered well, but there was something weird. He said there were some mechanical problems. Spark plugs and a fuel filter — and he was getting it fixed, but it wouldn't be ready in time. Maybe he was telling the truth. I was too exhausted to be sure about anything."

Without bothering to respond, Erick grabs his phone and punches one of the numbers on his speed dial.

"Hiya, Skeeter. You working on a van?"

Leaning closer, I hope I'm sending the "put it on speaker" vibe.

"Did anyone bring one in? Hmmm. Is there

anybody else in town who might be doing mechanic work on the side?"

Erick is clearly not picking up on my silent message. I point to the phone and mouth, "Speaker."

Nothing.

"You sure? Figured. That's why I called you first. Mmhmm. By the way, you think you can get me a school bus?"

They share a laugh. Not with me, though. I cross my arms and glare.

"No, nothing as elaborate as last time. Mitzy needs to drive her roller derby team to the bout tomorrow night. You sure? I knew I could count on you. Yeah. You got it. Thanks."

Erick lays his phone on the table, and I can't help but steal his thunder. "Two birds. One stone? Nobody in town is working on that van, and Skeeter can get a bus for tomorrow night."

He hops up, grabs his T-shirt from the back of his chair, and, much to my dismay, pulls it on, thereby ending my dinner and a *show*.

"Correct. Skeeter knew exactly which van I was talking about. Last time he worked on it was three weeks ago, when he replaced the spark plugs and the fuel filter. The thing was running perfectly and there would be no reason to take it in . . . unless—"

"Unless they didn't take it in. Unless — they're

hiding it because there's a human-sized dent in the front!"

"Correct again."

"I need to update Grams and the murder board." Turning on my toes, I race toward the door.

"Hey, am I invited?"

Pausing with one hand on the door handle, I open my mouth in shock. "Always. You're part of the gang now, Harper. I'm not sure what we're gonna do when you become sheriff, but we'll probably take a vote. Maybe we'll keep you in with some kind of honorary status."

He rakes his fingers through his hair, and those long, sexy bangs drape across one eye as he shakes his head. "Yeah. I still haven't wrapped my head around how I'm going to deal with all that."

"Don't give it a moment's thought. Conflict of interest with wife's PI business is Future Erick's problem."

He chuckles and crosses his arms in that yummy way that makes his biceps bulge.

With a huge, inclusive gesture, I call out, "Come on. We've got a murder to solve!"

CHAPTER 17

AFTER UPDATING THE MURDER BOARD and taking last-minute derby pointers from Grams, Erick and I head back to the walk-up.

Harper the Hero — I'm thinking about keeping that nickname for him — took care of securing a bus for my team. Skeeter said Artie promised to park it outside the warehouse tonight and leave the keys tucked in the visor.

That's how you know you live in a small town.

I send a quick text to Atlas that the bus has been secured and ask him what time we leave. He responds with a single word. "Noon."

Turning the screen to face Erick, I shrug and shake my head. "Not even a 'Thanks, Tipsy.'"

Erick bobs his head in a pattern that is neither

yes nor no. "You said he's the owner, and the coach, right?"

I bob my head in a decidedly affirmative pattern.

"Well, he's probably preoccupied with the bout. Lotta stuff on his mind, you know. Transporting the whole team, making sure he has all the supplies, hoping to win. It's a lot. Don't take it personally."

The corners of my mouth twitch upward, but I'm pretty sure both of us know the smile is superficial at best.

Erick should be well aware: I take everything personally. That's kind of my jam. It doesn't hurt anyone to say thank you. Two little words. Barely any effort. It used to drive me crazy when I worked at the coffee shop in Sedona and tourists would blow through with their entitled, out-of-town attitudes. Many of them failed to say thank you, and even more failed to tip. I get that tipping for everything has gotten out of hand, but even a small tip can make a difference to someone struggling to make it on minimum wage.

Erick's amused grin pushes in like a camera on a dolly shot, and suddenly we're nose-to-nose.

"Oops. What did I miss?"

My patient husband kisses the tip of my nose. "You better get some sleep, Moon. Tomorrow will be a big day. Are you sure you're ready for it?"

"Totally. As long as the game — I mean, the bout — doesn't last longer than three hours . . . I'm golden. My helmet ran out of juice at the end of the second practice today, and I took quite a spill."

His expression turns serious as he kneels down to check me for bruises. "You should've told me? Are you okay?"

"Yeah, the only thing truly injured was my pride. I sprawled out like a smashed spider and slid halfway across the floor. Several girls were yelling, 'Small fall.' Or maybe it was 'Fall small.' I don't know what that means."

My former-jock husband races to my aid. "Oh, it's a key part of derby. When you take a hit, if you go down, you want to fall forward as often as possible and pull your arms and legs in. That's falling small. There's a lot of action on the track, and if you leave your arms and legs sprawled out, someone might skate over them. Or fall on them. It's dangerous."

"Looks like somebody's bucking for an assistant coach job." As I'm chuckling, Erick fidgets nervously with his cuticles.

"Hey, what's going on? I know you're not trying to go undercover as a coach. Are you?!"

He waves his hands in the air like he's trying to clear invisible smoke.

"No. I got a hold of CC. As you know, he loves

sticking it to me. He said he'd be only too happy to keep an eye on my wife. That guy. A hopeless flirt."

Mischief twinkles in my gaze as I lean forward and whisper. "Looks like your blue eyes might be turning a little *green*, Harper."

He wraps his arms around my waist and pulls me close. "Jealousy is healthy. I'm not possessive. I don't try to control you. However, I'm always going to be on high alert when other guys ogle my woman."

A giggle escapes as I attempt an innocent nod. "Got it. But, just to be clear, you're not possessive. Right?"

He exhales softly and leans back. "I saw some pretty messed up domestic stuff when I was sheriff. That word, *possessive*, has a real negative connotation for me. I would never isolate you and cut you off from your support system. Those are the earmarks of an abuser."

Guilt drags across my face. "Oh, no. You would never — I'm so sorry. I was only kidding around."

He kisses my forehead. "I know. You better get yourself upstairs, put that helmet deep in the dark closet, take a shower, and hit the rack."

I pop a salute and head up the stairs.

At the top of the first flight, I look back, and it pleases me greatly to note that he's watching my progress with the unwavering stare of an apex predator.

Still got it.

Morning comes far too soon. Rolling out of bed, I march through the basics like a robot on a low battery. The smell of bacon sizzling two floors below puts a little pep in my step.

When I reach the kitchen, Grams tears across the room, glowing with excitement. "Today's the big day!"

Kicking out my curvy hip, I place a fist on it. "Who let *you* in?"

Her glow fades to a flicker, and I immediately regret my comment.

"Grams, I'm messing with you. I love that Erick invited you. I'm happy to see you, and I appreciate your excitement."

Her luminous face grins almost maniacally. "You're going to be fabulous! That helmet is amazing!"

"It is, isn't it?"

Erick places my breakfast on the table and returns to fill our coffee mugs. "Yeah, Silas is something else. I watched you trip and fall for almost five years. I never would've pictured you staying afloat on roller skates."

My mouth is too full for any kind of comeback. However, Grams giggles and Pyewacket offers his own commentary.

"RE-OW!" Game on!

At least my fiendish feline has some team spirit. "Now that's the stuff, Pyewacket."

Erick leaves for the PI office, and I send Grams and Pye to the apartment to keep working on the perfect European vacation. Which, amazingly, is still a surprise.

Time for a second — make that third — cup of coffee and a moment's peace before I head to the warehouse.

A firm knock at the front door spoils that plan.

"Was I expecting you?" Silas Willoughby stands on my front stoop with an expression that reminds me of the cat who swallowed the canary.

In an absolutely out-of-character maneuver, he does not wait for an invitation. Instead, he pushes past and walks directly toward the fireplace.

"Silas? What's going on?"

He steps close to me, and his energy carries an unusual crackle. "Are you quite certain we are alone?" The scent of stale tobacco and denture cream fills the narrow gap between us.

"Yes. I sent Grams and Pyewacket to the apartment, and I was about to head to the warehouse."

Silas sighs, but continues glancing in all the corners.

"You're kind of freaking me out. Are we in danger?"

He inhales sharply and paces in front of the hearth. "In all my born days, I never envisioned this moment."

I recognize a theatrical buildup when I see one. Crossing my arms, I step back and give him room to complete the performance.

"There were volumes . . . Volumes of notes. Rivail was a meticulous keeper of records."

"Rivail Gustafson? The tailor who—" I can't bring myself to mention the manner of his death. The man was an absolute wizard with a needle and thread. It wasn't until after his life had been taken that I learned he truly was a wizard. His whimsical hair and singsong voice will forever hold a special place in my heart.

"Indeed. His belongings came to me after he passed. I gave his journals a cursory read and stored them, along with the remainder of his possessions, in one of my spare rooms."

Spare rooms. There's an understatement. I don't dare interrupt Silas, but this man lives in the one and only Gothic mansion outside of Pin Cherry Harbor. He has more spare rooms than most people have used rooms.

"The message from Coraline Moon sent me delving into my previous research. There were loose threads of information everywhere. That was entirely Rivail's intention. At long last, I reached the final page of his final journal and read what stands as his last entry: 'Whenever I lose the source, I return to my humble origins. A bit of mending and darning refreshes the soul.'"

The milky fog in my mentor's eyes lifts, and they show a brilliant blue. His body positively quivers with excitement.

"Sorry. I'm not picking up what you're laying down. What's so special about that entry?"

Silas steeples his fingers and rests his jowly chin on the pointers.

Great. Lesson time. I have to figure this out for myself.

Centering myself, I reach out with my extrasensory perceptions.

Silas has something. Powerful. Now that I'm quiet and observant, I can sense this new energy in the room.

"Is Rivail's final message some kind of riddle?"

Silas claps his hands! "I knew it would come to you, Mizithra." His left hand fishes into one of the many hidden pockets in his old tweed jacket.

"His words sent me to his mother's sewing box. Secreted inside a darning egg—" When his hand reemerges, it is closed around a small but seemingly heavy object.

Leaning forward, I hold my breath in anticipation.

"What is it? What do you have?"

He opens his hands, and I sense the true power of the item in an instant. A hunched stone figure wearing the carved garments of a hermit, with an enormous right ear. "The Oracle? You found it?"

He smiles with a combination of satisfaction and reverence.

"Silas, do you know what this means?"

He harrumphs. "I suppose you shall tell me."

"I can bring my mother back. I can bring Coraline Moon back to this side of the veil. She can meet Erick, and you, and Odell, and Dad—" The thought of reuniting my mother with the man she never told of my existence stops me short.

My knees go weak, and I collapse onto the sofa. "Maybe she wouldn't want to meet Dad." He and my mother were a one-night stand, and she never bothered to track down the handsome out-of-towner who left her with much more than a warm memory of some Greek cheese. She happily named me after the dairy product that featured prominently in their "meet-cute," raised me on her own, and never said an unkind word about my biological father. But that doesn't mean she'd want to reunite. Blerg. Maybe Silas can offer a second opinion. "What do you think?"

Silas smooths his mustache and purses his lips. "I think an action of this magnitude requires careful thought. I shall place this relic in a secure location and give you time to ponder your decision."

With that, he turns and approaches the fireplace. He counts from the right — over two bricks to the left and down seven. Using the tip of the wrought-iron poker, he pushes firmly on that brick. It pops out, revealing a secret compartment. Silas places the Oracle of Return in the compartment and firmly pushes the brick into place.

"Um? Has that always been there?"

He walks away from me and replies softly, without direct eye contact. "When you asked for my help with sigils and wards during the construction, I made some additional provisions. I won't always be here and—"

Rushing toward my beloved curmudgeon, I throw my arms around his protesting form and blurt, "Don't say that! You're the second most important person in my life, Silas. Don't tell Grams."

He sputters and extracts himself from my bear hug. "Mizithra, you are one of a kind. It has been my absolute pleasure to make your acquaintance and assist you in developing your abilities. You must be realistic, my dear. Time marches on. For all of us, except your grandmother." His chuckle is bittersweet and brings tears to my cheeks.

"There has to be some relic, some object that will slow down time. Just for you. I want — I want my children to know you."

He spins on the well-worn heels of his loafers, and, for once, I've truly shocked the man.

"Is there something you wish to tell me?" His gaze falls to my abdomen.

"What? No. No. It just came up the other night, with Erick, and I wasn't sure how I felt about it until — until I thought about losing you. Promise me you'll delay the inevitable as long as possible."

"I shall do what is in my power to be done. In the meantime, you have a great deal to consider." He steps closer, takes my right hand, and kisses the back of my knuckles. "You're a treasure, young lady. I wish you all the best in your bout."

He shuffles toward the exit, as tears blur my vision. Silas quietly closes the door behind him, leaving me alone with my big thoughts.

I'm not a fan of time marching on.

CHAPTER 18

ONCE WE BOARD THE BUS, I grab one of the programs poking out of the coach's bag and review the
skater's names. I've heard most of them at practice,
so there are only a couple derby names on the roster
I can't place. As I'm about to ask about Barb Erica,
someone yells, "Barb! Sit here."

All right. Check.

There's no one else boarding the bus, and I still
don't see Celia Fate anywhere.

Leaning over the seat toward Betty Beware, I
ask what I think is an innocent question. "Where's
Celia Fate?"

The rowdy bus falls silent in a split second. All
eyes lock on Atlas as he boards the bus. His expression is soft and unconcerned. Not sure why the

mention of Celia got everyone's attention. But you know me: I like to poke the bear.

"Atlas, I was checking the roster, and I don't think Celia is here. Should we wait for her?"

His jaw tightens imperceptibly. Imperceptibly, if you only have five senses. My extra ones definitely clock the reaction.

"She got injured in our last bout. Celia's sitting this one out."

Weird. I don't remember anyone being injured at the bout at the community college. And from what I know about athletes, even the injured ones sit on the bench — if they're able. "Oh, that's too bad. I hope she gets better soon."

There was that muscle twitch in his jaw again. "Me too. Where are the keys?"

"Visor. You want me to drive?"

"I thought I was the only one who knew how to drive a stick. Was I wrong?" He tilts his head to the side like a confused cocker spaniel.

I hadn't noticed until that very moment that this bus had a manual transmission. The last time Erick got a bus for one of our capers, it was fortunately an automatic.

"Oh, I hadn't noticed. All yours."

Atlas grabs the keys, starts the bus, and pulls out of the parking lot.

We're on our way. I leave my gear bag in the

front seat and head toward the back of the bus. If I plan on pumping these gals for information, I need to be out of earshot of our coach.

The moment I flop onto the seat behind Cellblock Dee, her expression darkens.

I thought she liked me. Maybe I should move. As I glance around for an empty seat, her strong hand grips my arm and her voice, barely a whisper, warns me. "Don't ask questions. We have to do things. We don't talk about it. No questions. Érted?"

For some reason, her use of the Hungarian word for understand makes sense to me, and the correct response pops into my head. "Igen."

"You speak Hungarian?"

"A little, I guess." This is a new flavor of my language-related ability. But I'll take it. Silas is always muttering various alchemical phrases in other languages. I'd be more than happy to learn a few of my own. "Why won't anyone talk about Celia? I didn't see her get hurt at the bout."

Dee grips my arm so tight there's instantly the burn of interrupted circulation. "This is one of the things. No questions."

Twisting my arm free, I rub the finger marks furiously and glare. "What gives? I thought you were my friend?"

A look of pain flashes across her face, and she

absently rubs the crown with the tilted cross tattoo on her left thigh.

My attention shifts. "Why do so many of the gals have that tattoo?"

The sudden subject change confuses her. "Sacred Crown of Hungary." Her tone is clipped and soft. "They mark us." Her gaze falls to the floor.

"Dee, I am truly a friend. You can tell me anything."

The muscles in her jaw clench. "No friends. Too dangerous."

"Why is it dangerous?"

She bites her lip and looks toward Betty, but she continues. "The team has expenses. Travel. Medical. Lots of money."

"All right. Why is that dangerous?"

A flash of terror ripples over her with such fury it makes my mouth go dry. Reaching toward her, I place my hand on top of hers and attempt to send her some of the calming energy Silas Willoughby has shared with me — too many times to count.

Her breathing slows and her shoulders relax.

Dee leans toward me. "We sell things. Sometimes Atlas, he buy things. We sell these things to make this money."

It worked! I silently thank my mentor for his endless but patient lessons.

The hairs on the back of my neck tingle. Not sure I want to hear the answer to my next question, but I have to ask. "What kinds of things?"

"This." She rummages in her gear bag and pulls out a bundle wrapped in plastic.

I don't need street smarts to hear the word floating through my psychic mind. *Meth.* Crapballs.

"Dee, I can't sell drugs. I won't."

She grips my arm again. This time it feels more pleading than painful. "Don't make him angry. Please."

Her fear is palpable. So, Atlas Hahn isn't the easy-going, happy-go-lucky guy he pretends to be. Good to know.

Once I get Cellblock Dee talking, it's like water spilling from a broken dam. There's no stopping her story.

"We pay to come to America. They take money and passport in Budapest. Put us on a bus. From bus to boat. Then we end up here."

"Why did they take your passport? Did they take you from Hungary illegally . . ."

"This is why we sell the kristály-metadin."

It doesn't take a psychic to translate that phrase. Crystal meth. That's what must be in the little plastic packets I saw in my mood ring.

Dee continues. "To get passport cost money. To

pay for this passport and to live, we have to make money."

"But when are you done? When have you paid enough to get your passport back?" She's describing indentured servitude, but there's a big red light flashing in my psychic brain, and the only thing it says is human trafficking.

"I don't know this. No one is free — yet." Her attempt to add a hopeful twist falls flat. She doesn't believe any of them will ever be free.

The oppressed foster kid in me wants to march to the front of the bus and punch Atlas Hahn in the face. But that's not enough.

Now, I totally believe Boomer when he told Erick and me that his girlfriend had nothing to do with Jason Samson's murder.

What better way to gather evidence against this Hahn character than by going along with his scam? He doesn't know I have my phone. I can take pictures of the drugs and record him telling us what to sell. When Erick and Skeeter find the team van for the Rink Rashers, we can add murder to the growing list of charges against this scumbag.

"I don't want to make trouble for you guys. I'll go along with it today, but I'll probably have to quit the team."

Dee loosens her grip on my arm and sinks back

against the slashed green-vinyl seat. "I wish to quit. But how? Where do I go?"

Where indeed? Hahn holds all the cards. He must have their passports on the bus, but these poor girls don't know that. I hate everything about this. If only I could text Erick, but I can't risk Hahn seeing me use my phone. I'm certain he's the reason none of the other gals have phones.

The best thing I can do right now is use my time on the bus wisely. I spend the rest of our trip gathering information about each of the women. All but two are from Hungary. Those two are from Croatia. They were scammed into this mess in a town called Split right before everyone was loaded on a cargo ship.

The absent Celia Fate is from Budapest and has a six-year-old son back home in Józsfeváros. She had been living with her mother and working as a tour guide. She went to one of the city's popular, but dangerous, post-war ruin bars for a friend's birthday and happened to flash her passport as identification to buy drinks. Someone slipped something into her beer. She woke up in handcuffs on a bus heading for the Adriatic Sea. Barb Erica says Celia always worries about her son, but she wouldn't let herself cry. Barb's terrified voice shakes and she struggles to swallow. For the first time, I feel their collective fear.

Trapped. Hopeless. Deceived.

I casually bounce my way seat by seat back toward my gear bag, reassuring all the women that I won't cause any trouble and I'll skate my best in the bout.

When Atlas pulls the bus to the curb in front of Crooks Bay High School, all the skaters grab their gear bags and unload.

Cellblock Dee takes charge. There's no sign of the fearful, hesitant woman who confessed dark secrets to me on our journey north.

"Head to the gym. We warm up now."

"Copy that."

Crooks Bay high school reminds me of small-town America in the 1950s, or, more accurately, the Reese Witherspoon classic, *Pleasantville*.

Everything is in its place, and I can almost see the cheerleaders in their long poodle skirts and three-quarter sleeve sweaters with their favorite beau's pin over their hearts.

I head inside with the rest of the gals, but my breath catches when CC, Erick's Canadian Mountie buddy in his glorious red-and-black uniform, smiles and nods at me from the lobby.

Shaking my head with as much subtlety as I can muster, I hope he knows better than to acknowledge me.

His dashing smile fades, and he instantly shifts

his gaze to a group of high schoolers getting rowdy by a vending machine.

Whew. That was close.

The crowd in the gymnasium consists of locals and a handful of diehard Pin Cherry fans who made the drive. Along the top of the twenty-five-foot-high walls, one championship banner after another nearly completes a circle around the gym.

At first glance, one might assume that the sports programs at this school are stellar. Something in the back of my brain flutters, and a different explanation shimmers into solid form as though it's been beamed from the deck of the starship *Enterprise.*

There's no competition in this ultra-rural district. Whoever the Crooks Bay Marauders — their mascot is emblazoned on the gym wall — play in their various sporting events provides little competition.

Inside the gymnasium, there's no fancy sport court like we had in Pin Cherry. Locals have carefully taped the outline of the track and placed pivot and jammer lines appropriately. Looks like Rink Rasher drug money can finance some classy accoutrements. The thought turns my stomach.

I follow my team to the bench assigned to us, and hope that the Crooks Bay Rollers are as bad as they look.

They only have ten skaters. That means some

of their gals are going to be skating without any re-lief for ninety minutes. If nothing else, we should be able to outlast them purely by having the ability to swap out our skaters and get fresh jammers on the rink.

Listen to me! I definitely sound like an old pro.

CHAPTER 19

ERICK

WITH CC KEEPING an eye on Mitzy, it's time for Boomer and me to find this missing van. We call in the expertise of Birch County's vehicular Wikipedia.

Skeeter pulls up out front of the walk-up in his tow truck, and Boomer and I slink out in our all-black attire. When I open the passenger door, the expert mechanic is already doubled over with laughter.

"What's funny?"

He points to Boomer and me. "This ain't a jewel heist. I don't need cat burglars. We're gonna be checking a few remote locations where I've previously found abandoned cars, and then we'll probably end up at the junkyard — that I own. What in the Sam Hill are you two plannin'?"

Before I can come up with a clever reply, Boomer calls "shotgun" and I end up wedged between the two of them on the bench seat. Despite trying to protect my left knee from the 4-on-the-floor stick shift, I take two hits before we're even off First Avenue.

Skeeter drives with utter disregard for the rules of the road. I may no longer be in law enforcement, but Boomer is a sworn officer of the Birch County Sheriffs. If he's not speaking up, I'm not going to be the wet blanket.

"Hang on, boys." With that simple phrase, Skeeter jams the headlight switch off and turns down a sketchy dirt road. The moon is almost full, and, in nature's darkness, it provides adequate light for someone familiar with the route.

The road comes to a sudden dead-end. A rusted, square-body pickup truck with a busted axle lies abandoned under the heavy branches of a huge pine.

Skeeter points. "I'll come back and get you tomorrow, little lady."

Boomer chuckles beside me. "You really do know about every car in this county, Skeeter."

Our driver exhales with satisfaction. "Folks tell me I got a sixth sense about these things. Pshaw. Just doin' what I love."

We hit up three more of Skeeter's secret locations and come up empty-handed.

My shoulders sag. "Now what?"

Skeeter jams the shifter into reverse and cracks the side of my knee. I wince and angle toward Boomer.

"You trying to make a move on me, Harper?"

Leaning close, I play into Boomer's concern. "You'd know if I was." That shuts him right up.

Skeeter pops the headlights back on as we hit the main road. "We head to the junkyard, boys. Twenty-five acres of free-range metal. Hard to say if anyone's joined the herd in the last few days."

The master mechanic drives past the main entrance to his junkyard and shop, then continues down a seemingly endless fence line. Eventually, I can make out a dirt road partially obscured by low-hanging tree branches. He makes a hard left and heads into the darkness.

His headlights reflect off the eyes of a fox or two, and a doe with two fawns. Just when I'm about to throw in the towel and ask him to turn around, the high beams illuminate a van deep in the snowy ditch and partially obscured by freshly cut pine branches.

Skeeter stops while Boomer and I bail out the side, weapons drawn.

Using a standard tactical approach, I head for the driver's door while he covers me.

When I move around to get a clear look into the front seats of the vehicle, it appears empty. I pop the door, scan the front of the vehicle, and call out, "Clear."

Boomer pops open the rear double doors, looks under the seats, climbs in to check the bench seats, and responds, "Clear."

With the imminent danger out of the way, I motion for Skeeter to join us. He carries a massive battery-powered lamp and blasts its rays on the front of the van.

The three of us share a collective "whoa" as he illuminates the human-sized dent — and the dried-blood evidence.

He pops the trunk lever and uses a crowbar to open the hood. "You see that shiny new fuel filter?" He points the bright light and gestures for us to take a gander. "That's my handiwork, boys. This 1991 GMC Rally G-series manual-transmission van belongs to Atlas Hahn. I'd stake my reputation on it."

I turn to Skeeter. "We need—"

"On it, chief."

He returns to his vehicle and radios in the find. Paulsen and her team will be here soon enough. In the meantime, Boomer and I carefully search for any clue as to who was driving this vehicular weapon.

Coming up empty-handed, a larger concern looms. I grab my phone and call CC.

No answer.

"Skeeter, how fast can you get us back to town?"

He picks at his greasy fingernails and grins. "Let's find out, eh?"

A rooster tail of dust and gravel spits out behind the truck as Skeeter puts the hammer down. He downshifts and takes the right-hand turn without touching the brakes.

We're flying past the city limit sign when flashing lights and sirens pass us, heading the opposite way.

Skeeter doesn't slow down for a second.

Boomer whoops and hollers. "Dang, son. Paulsen is going to lose her mind."

Our skilled driver sniffs sharply. "Nah, I've got a few favors to call in."

We all chuckle as Skeeter hits the brakes hard in front of the bookshop and checks his phone.

"Beat my own record by two minutes and thirty-five seconds."

Boomer and I shake our heads in awed silence.

"Go on! Get out, boys. I gotta get back there and tow that rig into town for the *current* sheriff."

He doesn't say anything, but I can tell by the tone of his voice that he's heard about my plans to run in November.

"Thanks for your help. I owe you, buddy."

Skeeter shakes his head. "If the rumors are true, you've already paid me back."

With a quick salute, he flips a U-turn and heads back toward the junkyard and the van.

Tossing my phone on the counter, I exhale my frustration. "I can't get ahold of CC. If Atlas Hahn, or one of the derby girls, was driving that van—"

Boomer puts a hand on my shoulder. "Let's hit the road, Harper. If you take a page from Skeeter's book, you can get us to Canada in no time."

"I'll need my passport. What about you?"

He flashes his badge and grins.

"Yeah, those things come in handy." I grab the Nova keys and head upstairs for my passport.

Yanking my top dresser drawer open in the darkness, I rifle through fist-sized balls of paired socks.

"Where the heck is my passport?" I always keep it in this drawer. Now is not the—

"Ree-OW!"

Mitzy's not here to interpret, but that doesn't sound good. Flicking on the light, I walk toward the powerful caracal seated on the bed.

Under his left paw . . . "One step ahead, as usual." I retrieve my passport from his clawed clutches and turn to leave.

"R-OW!"

All my years on the force help me understand exactly what he means. "She's in trouble, isn't she?"

"Reow." Can confirm.

That one I know. "I'll bring her back in one piece — if it's the last thing I do."

Taking the stairs two at a time, I race out to the Nova and the engine roars to life.

Boomer calls in favors from every deputy he knows to clear the way for our run for the border.

All I can think is how much danger Mitzy could be in. Don't do anything stupid, Moon.

Who am I kidding?

The best I can hope is to arrive before the stupid thing she does becomes irreversible.

CHAPTER 20

MY TEAM'S ALL WARMED UP, but derby in Canada is a little different. The Crooks Bay announcer doesn't have a special booth or a flair for the dramatic. He sits behind a rickety folding table in front of the bleachers. His announcement of the starting lineup is bland and offers no opportunity for skaters to show off. The names are fired like bullets out of a semi-automatic weapon, and no one makes a move toward the track.

Got it. Apparently, we're not in Kansas anymore.

In keeping with the Wizard of Oz theme, I ponder the true motivation of our man behind the curtain. What got Atlas Hahn involved in trafficking young women from Eastern Europe? The obvious answer is money. How much money does it take to blacken someone's soul to such a void that they can accept this fallout?

Apparently, I'm not built to understand.

The whistle blows, and I skate onto the track. My first official jam, in my first official bout.

A couple of the gals slap hands with me as they skate to the bench, and I take my place behind the pivot. The whistle blows and we move. A double whistle follows and the jammers advance. Our jammer easily outskates the Crooks Bay Rollers', and with the help of our blockers, she continues to lap the opposing team until the jam ends.

When I look up, the scoreboard shows twenty-six points.

Wow! This game is going to be a blowout. I wonder if Hahn will tell us to go easy on them at halftime?

The first half continues, and although Crooks Bay gets forty-five points on the board, we are closing in on one hundred.

The teams skate to opposing benches for the halftime break.

Atlas seems pleased with himself. "Good job, ladies. This game will end on time and we'll make a quick stop before we head home. Any questions?"

My teammates instantly shake their heads.

They rise as one and skate toward an exit. I'm late off the bench, but I quickly catch up.

Cellblock Dee grips the studded belt around my waist and pulls me toward her. "Now we sell. Be quick."

"I don't have anything to sell. Atlas didn't give me any kristály-metadin."

Her face floods with disbelief, but she exhales and nods. "Stick with me."

I nod once as the team skates outside behind the gymnasium.

The hairs on the back of my neck stand on end. Was this what was happening in Pin Cherry? Maybe Jason Samson wasn't the goody two shoes everyone thought. Clearly, his family was in financial trouble. If he was cutting into Hahn's drug territory, retaliation would be swift. A man with Hahn's soulless vibe wouldn't draw the line at killing a teenager. He wouldn't draw a line anywhere.

Locals drift in and out of the narrow alley behind the school, and the ladies quickly sell their packets and shove cash into their brassieres.

Betty Beware glances at her watch. Not for the first time; I imagine the controlling grip of Atlas Hahn is why none of them have phones. She announces, "Time to get back."

The gals wrap up their sales, and we all skate into the gymnasium.

Atlas lifts his chin and narrows his gaze. Betty and Cellblock give affirmative nods, and his shoulders relax as he sits on the bench.

What a piece of work. Maybe I should say, a piece of human *debris*. I have pictures of the transactions and even a recording of one of the sales. What I don't have is Atlas directing everyone to take part in illegal activities.

Hopefully, I can trick him into saying something on the way home.

Checking my battery, I'm pleased to see I have eighty percent charge. At least that's one thing I don't have to worry about. I can turn the recording feature on, click the screen to black, and hide the phone back in the waistband of my booty shorts. That leaves the tricky task of getting Atlas to incriminate himself.

No worries. I've never been afraid of a challenge.

Canadian Mountie CC enters through the double doors at the end of the gymnasium and casually glances around. His steely gaze pauses on me, and I nod once. He exhales and shakes his head with disappointment.

I have no idea how much Erick has told him, but I hope he understands my message.

Scanning the opposing bench, I notice a scruffy-looking guy in a blue puffer vest. Hold the phone! I recognize him! He was buying from Mona Madness.

The entire opposing team took drugs during halftime?! Oh. My. Gosh. This isn't going to be the runaway bout I imagined.

It only takes half an hour for them to catch up. Now, with every jam, we're skating for our lives. Hahn is angry and pacing on the sideline. He's shouting at the girls in Hungarian, and my extra language ability gives me enough information to tell me it's not encouragement he's hurling at the skaters.

There are two minutes left on the clock, and we're down by twenty-eight points. This is our last chance.

Cellblock Dee skates over and hands me the helmet cover with a star emblazoned on either side. "Why are you giving me the panties? I'm not a jammer."

She swallows with difficulty, glances toward Atlas, and shoves down the cover firmly into my hands. "You jam now."

Oh, I get it. They want the new girl to take the fall if they lose. Great. I've gotta pump this guy for information and try to get him to incriminate himself on the record. On top of all that, he's going to be furious with me for the entire ride back to Pin Cherry Harbor.

"You guys are making a mistake." I grab the helmet cover, tug it on top of my helmet, and skate toward the jammer line.

The Crooks Bay jammer is wild-eyed and jumpy. I'm not sure she even knows what she's doing anymore. I stand behind the pack, ready to go — with one skate on the rink and the other toe-stop primed for the push-off.

Their blockers seem to have grown six inches and fifty pounds in size.

Whistle one. The pack rolls.

Double whistle.

I'm off the line in a flash. Cutting to the inside, I execute an apex jump, slam into their pivot, and take lead jammer status. Now, I skate for my life.

Their wired-up jammer is hot on my tail, so I bend my knees and swing my right arm hard as I crossover my skates and round the curve.

When I approach the pack, Betty Beware and Silence of the Jams open a hole. I reach out and grab Betty's outstretched arm as she whips me through the gap.

Out front once again, I skate hard. No part of me can believe the power of this helmet. I feel confident. Stable. Like I could skate forever.

When I come up on the pack again, Betty attempts to repeat her move, but the opposing team blocks her hard and sends her sprawling off the track.

They seem to be setting up some kind of trap for me.

As I attempt to reach out psychically and see if I can get a feel for what they're up to, my perceptions are totally blocked. Whatever's going on with this helmet—?

Someone hits me from behind and knocks me off my skates and into the center of the track. They're sent to the penalty box for back blocking, but it's up to me to fall small, jump up, and regain my advantage.

Mona Madness blasts two of their skaters off the track with one astounding hip check. I fly by and grab a few more points.

When I went down, their jammer was able to pass me. We're tied one eighty-three each. There are fifteen seconds left on the clock.

Crouching farther and pumping my outside arm as hard as humanly possible, I feel like I'm grabbing another gear on the racetrack. Flying by their jammer, I catch up with the pack and get two points on the board before the final buzzer blows.

My teammates leap off the bench and skate toward us. One of the diehard Pin Cherry fans lets loose a roll of toilet paper as the handful of loyal followers clap louder than a crowd ten times their size.

The overall mood is joyful, and even Hahn seems back to his old self. His feathered hair flows in the breeze as he walks up and down the bench, congratulating us. "Good job, ladies. We'll stop for dinner. Then a bit of business, and we all head home."

He's got me wondering what that bit of business might be. I don't like the sound of it.

As we head out, Atlas is called over by CC. My heart is in my throat, and I refuse to make eye contact.

Their exchange looks friendly, and I sincerely hope CC doesn't blow my one chance at getting the evidence we need.

We all walk back to the bus and wait for Atlas to join us. As I wander around, muffled sounds reach my ears.

I can't make them out, so I reach out with my extra abilities and sense something or someone trapped under the bus.

As I kneel to get a better reading, my head throbs with pain, and the name Celia Fate blasts against my skull.

Someone — pretty sure it's Celia — is trapped under the bus. Tied up inside the huge luggage compartments between the front and rear axles.

The psychic hits are coming in hard and fast.

Atlas needs to get rid of her.

Her breathing is labored.

She's dehydrated — and maybe hypothermic.

Celia must know something about the murder.

There's no time for me to set her free. Looking around for anything that I could use to let her know I'm trying to help, I see a broken soda bottle.

That jagged edge is just what I need. I wedge it in front of the rear bus tire and hope that the leak is slow enough that Atlas won't suspect foul play.

Atlas Hahn arrives, and we all load onto the bus. My heart is racing. I have no idea how to get out of this mess.

The bus pulls away from the curb, and I hope I'm the only one who hears the strange crunching hiss from the right rear tire.

We're about ten or fifteen miles outside of town, in utter blackness, in the middle of nowhere, when the tire starts flapping.

Atlas swears in Hungarian, and the entire energy in the bus shifts to one of terror.

He yanks the steering wheel, and the bus bounces along the gravel shoulder. Hahn turns off the engine and gets to his feet. "Tipsy, you help me change the flat. Your bus. Your problem."

Real nice guy. "You got it."

For some reason, I grab my helmet and strap it on. Doesn't make sense to me, but I've gotten to a point where I don't question my intuition.

He laughs as I stomp down the steps. "I don't need you to skate around while I change the tire. You don't need a helmet."

Attempting a casual tone, I toss back a response. "You lose eighty percent of your heat through your head. I just want to stay warm."

Seeming to accept my explanation, he motions for me to slide under the rear of the bus to get the tire and jack. The area he indicated is behind the large compartments. There's no way I'm going to tip my hand. I slither under without question.

Making a gesture with my hand to close off my psychic receptors, I have to block any messages from Celia. If I react to something now, it could ruin everything.

As I'm working with the large pry bar/lug nut wrench, I start my interrogation. It's perfect that Atlas is behind me, since my phone hides in the back of my waistband and is recording everything.

"Why do you have the skaters sell drugs at halftime?"

His energy shifts from casual team owner to menacing thug in a flash.

"How about you mind your own business?"

"If you want me to be part of it, it is my business. All I want is an explanation."

He yanks the bar from my hand and cracks me solidly on the skull.

Despite the protection of my helmet, everything goes dark.

CHAPTER 21

INCESSANT SHIVERING FINALLY BRINGS me back to consciousness. Waking in complete darkness in the ditch beside an unfamiliar road is a whole new brand of terrifying.

How did my plan turn into a total dumpster fire?

Pushing myself into a seated position, I slowly remove my cracked helmet and feel across my skull for any damp patches that could indicate injury or concussion.

Shockingly, my skull feels intact. I can't say the same for my one-of-a-kind alchemically enhanced helmet. Not sure whether Silas will be disappointed it was destroyed while in my possession or thrilled that it saved my life.

A full body shiver violently contracts all my muscles.

Time to use my super brain to come up with solutions. I can probably walk fifteen miles. The movement would get my circulation going and fend off hypothermia.

However, Celia is in immediate danger. I mean — How long was I out? What if it's too late? A disembodied re-ow reminding me of my human inadequacies immediately brings an image of my cell phone to mind. Grabbing the phone from my waistband, I'm pleased to see it's undamaged.

The recording app is still running, and it looks like twenty-three minutes and some change have passed.

A rough calculation of drive time, and the flat tire incident that left me incapacitated on the roadside, and I'd say Atlas Hahn has approximately a three-minute head start.

There are two numbers that I call when the *BLEEP* hits the fan. Speed dial one: *Harper the Hero* is the winner at this moment.

"Mitzy! What's going on?" There's tension constricting my husband's voice, and also, there seems to be a significant amount of background noise. It almost sounds like—

"Are you driving?"

"Yeah. We're on our way to intercept the bus

and extract you before things go south. Boomer's got shotgun."

I'm not sure I want to know if that's a literal shotgun, or he's simply riding in the front passenger seat. "Um. We're in a good news, bad news situation, Harper. Which do you want first?"

Boomer calls out before Erick can answer, "Let's have the good news, Moon."

"The good news is I self-extracted. The bad news is I'm on the side of the road in the middle of nobody-cares-nowhere, and Celia Fate is tied underneath the school bus headed to who knows where!"

Erick attempts a lighthearted laugh, but it's obvious that he's more than a little worried.

"Sit tight. It looks like we're about five minutes from intercepting you. We got held up at the border and lost some time. We'll grab you and then head out and get that bus."

"How do you know—?" Once again, my abilities provide the answer I didn't know I needed. "You've been tracking me? Is there a tracking app on my phone like I'm some kind of delinquent teenager?"

My husband exhales with the patience of Job. "Can you blame me, Moon? We both know you get in trouble way more than any delinquent teen."

I don't care for the shared chuckle that follows.

"Fine. Let's see what that muscle car baby of

yours can do. Hahn's got a three-minute jump on us. Celia will be dead before we can help her if you don't get the lead out, Harper." Before the call ends, his eight-cylinder beast of an engine roars to life, and Boomer lets out a WOOT that would shame an Indy 500 fan.

In less than a minute, I see headlights on the horizon. Thirty-five seconds later, my chariot awaits.

Boomer hops out, does the honorable thing by jumping into the backseat, and I ride shotgun — the seat, not the firearm.

Erick reaches across and squeezes my knee firmly. "I don't suppose you know where that bus is headed?"

The unspoken question is: Can I psychically reach out and track this maniac, Atlas Hahn? Boomer doesn't need to know all of my deep, dark secrets. Thankfully, Erick is keeping things discreet.

"Let me think . . ." Taking a deep breath, I reach out with everything I've got and try to connect to Celia, Betty, or Dee. Since I got zero cooperation from Atlas before he tried to kill me, I hardly think that will serve as my way in now.

Wrong again!

The unhinged energy of Atlas Hahn slugs into my gut. I'm seeing through his eyes. Road sign. Customs and Border Protection 41 km.

"He's headed to the border. Maybe you guys passed him and you didn't realize."

Erick glances over his shoulder at Boomer, and they both shake their heads. "No way. It's a narrow two-lane highway. The only way we would have missed him is if he wasn't on the main road. Is there anything else you can tell me?"

Sinking into the quiet place within, another sign rips past Hahn's field of vision. "Provincial 608."

Erick reaches for his phone, but Boomer calls out, "I've already got it on GPS, Sheriff."

Twisting in my seat, I glance at Boomer. "He told you?"

Boomer nods enthusiastically. "Best news I've had all year."

He fires off directions to Erick like a copilot in a rally race.

We're traveling at a high rate of speed and only braking when absolutely necessary. I've got one hand wound through my seatbelt for extra security, and the other pushing firmly against the dash.

Boomer calls out the next turn, and Erick replies, "Good thing we put that sway bar under this baby."

Boomer chuckles. "No doubt. No doubt."

As the dirt road straightens out, the dim tail-lights of what can only be a school bus emerge in front of us. Erick stomps the gas pedal and shouts to Boomer, "Take a look and see if I have that lone cherry back there."

"10-4."

A moment later, Boomer hands up a single red light. Erick steers with one hand as he yanks out the cigarette lighter and plugs in the "cherry." Switching hands, he rolls down the window and throws the magnetic-based flashing red light on the roof.

The brake lights flash once on the bus, but then the taillights attempt to put distance between us.

Thankfully, buses aren't built for high-speed chase.

Erick gets as close as he dares and shouts, "Any ideas?"

"Not a one. There's a woman tied up in the huge baggage compartment under that bus. If we push Atlas, and he loses control of that bus, she's dead. Not to mention all the ladies sitting inside without seatbelts."

Boomer puts a hand on Erick's shoulder. "You better back off. Call CC and have the Mounties set up a roadblock. We'll fall back and keep an eye on them."

Erick pounds his fist on the steering wheel but nods his head in agreement. "Yeah. You're right. Can't risk anyone's life." He grabs his phone and calls in another favor from his favorite Canadian Mountie.

As the tension dissipates and we slip into surveillance mode, Erick's shoulders loosen.

"So how'd you end up on the side of the road, Moon? What were you doing to piss off the boss?" Boomer's crass question hangs in the air.

"I discovered the woman under the bus while we were waiting for Atlas after the bout. We won, by the way."

Erick rolls his head back. "Not really the point right now."

"Just saying." I wish they were more interested in hearing about the winning play. "Anyway, I didn't have time to free her, so I grabbed a broken bottle and wedged it against the tire. When we got a flat a few miles down the road, he had to pull over. Hahn volunteered me to help. While I was changing the tire, I asked him why he was making the skaters sell drugs at halftime."

Erick hangs his head and wipes one hand across his furrowed brow.

"Don't lecture me, Harper. I know. I know it wasn't the best approach." Shrugging my shoulders, I glance at Boomer for support, but he mirrors Erick's body language.

"Atlas grabbed the huge lug nut wrench from my hand and cracked me over the head. My helmet protected me." Glancing down at the cleaved head-gear between my feet, a spasm of worry constricts the muscles in my stomach.

"You were wearing your helmet?" Boomer leans forward.

"Yeah, I don't know why. Something made me put it on before I got off the bus."

Erick once again reaches across and squeezes my knee. "Let's be extra grateful for that *something,* right?"

"Copy that." Pulling out my phone, I scroll back to the recording. "When I woke up, I was kinda disoriented for a minute, then I remembered I had my phone in my waistband. And I recorded this."

Pushing play on the recording and cranking up the volume, Boomer and Erick nod in unison. Erick says, "It's inadmissible, but we might be able to use it to pry some type of confession out of Atlas."

Boomer nods. "For sure. For sure. What innocent guy cracks a chick over the head for no reason?"

My loyal hubby glances into the rearview mirror and shakes his head. "Let's refer to my wife by her name. Got it?"

Boomer chuckles. "Right. Who cracks Mitzy over the head for no reason?"

The bus ahead slows, and I assume Hahn sees the impending roadblock to the south.

Erick tightens his grip on the wheel. "Stay frosty. He might try to turn that thing around to avoid the roadblock."

Boomer pats Erick on the shoulder. "Too bad your buddy didn't send us some backup from the north, too."

If you've ever watched the *Lord of the Rings*, and you've seen that moment when Gandalf appears in the east with the riders of Rohan — well, you know exactly how the three of us feel. A sea of headlights burst over the horizon behind us and our one-man pursuit suddenly becomes awash with Canadian Mounties, border patrol, and a few law-enforcement agencies I don't recognize.

Erick glances at Boomer, and they share a smug expression. Harper adds, "Looks like the FBI and ICE. I don't think Atlas Hahn will ever see the light of day again."

My celebratory smile fades faster than the flavor of Fruit Stripe gum. "Celia! She's under that bus!"

CHAPTER 22

WITHOUT A THOUGHT for their own safety, Erick and Boomer leap out of the Nova.

I hurry along in their wake.

Erick kneels beside the bus, cranks the handle on the huge baggage compartment door, and yanks it open. He reaches out his right hand. "Spyderco."

Speaking a language known only to them, Boomer grabs a large folding knife clipped to his front pocket and hands it down.

My husband flicks it open with one slick movement and wriggles into the dark steel box.

Seconds later, he's sliding out with an unconscious woman in his arms. He looks at Boomer and shouts, "Chopper. Now."

Boomer flies into action.

He leans into the open trunk of one of the multitude of law enforcement vehicles and grabs two flares.

Running to the field beside the road, he ignites the flares and waves them to and fro. I'm no expert, but there seems to be a pattern.

One of the two helicopters overhead veers toward Boomer's signal.

He continues to wave the flares with more rapid gestures, and within seconds, the helo makes a landing in the field.

Erick surges forward with Celia. There's a brief exchange, but Erick gets the bird back in the air before trouble intervenes.

The FBI swoops in and attempts to take over, but Erick holds his ground.

"That woman was in critical condition. If she doesn't get immediate medical care, we'll have another death on our hands.

A young agent with the standard issue earpiece attempts to throw his weight around. "You have no jurisdiction here. I'll have your badge for that."

CC rushes to his buddy's aid. "To be clear, Agent, it's you who have no jurisdiction in Canada. We stand behind the decision to take a critical patient to the trauma center."

The blustering agent sucks in an angry breath as he prepares to continue his ego trip, but Erick cuts him off. "Atlas Hahn is wanted for Murder

One in my county. I'd say that trumps whatever you've got on the blotter."

A veteran agent steps forward. "Sheriff Harper? I remember my guys working with you on that train robbery case. Why don't we have a quick chat and sort this out?"

Erick, the senior FBI agent, Boomer, and CC have a lengthy discussion, but eventually, Harper the Hero wins them over. They clear the roadblock, and Boomer is allowed to drive the bus with the skaters through.

I sidle up next to Boomer and whisper, "There's a metal box with all their passports under the driver's seat."

Boomer scrunches up his face with suspicion, and I have to head off any questions.

When in doubt, lie it out. "I saw Hahn access them when we crossed the border."

He nods and hops aboard, calmly explaining the situation to the ladies as he closes the doors.

The FBI gets custody of Hahn — for human trafficking and drug smuggling — but he will also face the murder charge in Pin Cherry. Turns out it was *Hahn* who was being tracked by "them." I think even Alanis Morissette would agree that's ironic.

Immigration and Customs Enforcement (ICE) was eager to get their hands on the ladies, but

Boomer made a solid case for them all being material witnesses in the murder.

Celia was the one exception. The helo is taking her back to the Canadian Regional Trauma Centre, and everyone seems to be on board with that decision.

"Erick, I don't feel comfortable leaving her all alone in Canada. I think ICE will take her the minute she's been stabilized. I'm going to call Silas about the immigration issues, and then we need to go back to the hospital."

My husband smiles and nods. "Were you actually reading my mind, or is this just one of those husband-and-wife link-ups?"

My jaw slackens, and the color drains from my face. "I never. I promised—"

He slings an arm around my shoulders. "Hey, I'm joking around. I know you would never use your powers on me."

"Yeah. Thanks. I guess I'm more shook up than I thought."

He gently brushes the top of my head. "How's your noggin?"

"I want to say I'm okay." Lifting my hands, I offer a noncommittal gesture. "I mean, it hurts. But I didn't feel any blood or anything. The helmet is totally trashed, but at least it protected me."

"Remind me to buy Silas Willoughby an extra batch of alchemist's salt, or whatever he's into."

I chuckle at the thought of Erick attempting to buy Silas Willoughby an alchemical gift as we load into the Nova and head back toward Crooks Bay.

"Guess my derby days are over." The pieces of the helmet between my feet lie as useless ruins.

"Who knows? Maybe you can keep going to practices. Sure seemed like you enjoyed it."

My heart goes out to the women whom I had bonded with on the track. "What about the team?! There's no one to coach them and—"

Erick grips the steering wheel and shakes his head. "You better call Silas. The first thing we need to worry about is how we protect them from deportation."

"Copy that." Putting my phone on speaker, I call my wise mentor. "Sorry to bother you so late, Mr. Willoughby."

"Fear not. I am deep in the bowels of *De Praestigiis Daemonum*. How may I assist you?"

After a brief recap of the situation, carefully skipping over the cracked helmet, I get to the meat of my message. "So, Erick and I are headed back to the hospital to look after Celia Fate —her real name is Csilla Galler. And we'll need some legal protection to bring her back to Pin Cherry Harbor."

"An intriguing conundrum. I shall consult my

notes and contact you with instructions. Was it your understanding that Boomer was heading to Broken Rock or Pin Cherry?

Erick pipes up. "He knows the ladies all live in Pin Cherry. As much as it pains him, he's taking them to Paulsen to give their statements."

"A wise choice. I shall meet him at the station and see that these women are properly represented. Some of them may wish to return to their country."

That thought hadn't even crossed my mind. "This is why we pay you the big bucks, Silas."

He harrumphs. "I don't remember big bucks, as you say, being involved. I intend to assist these women from a place of basic humanitarian kindness."

"Apologies, Mr. Willoughby."

"Anything further, Mizithra?"

Blerg. Formal name territory. "Any women wanting to return to Europe will have all their expenses covered by the Duncan Moon Philanthropic Foundation. Also, if we can figure out some way to keep that roller derby team alive, for the women who are staying, I think they enjoy skating."

"Perhaps. And what about you? Do you enjoy skating?"

He knows. He always knows! "I did. Unfortunately, there was a minor accident when my head had an unscheduled meeting with a giant lug nut wrench. The helmet saved me, but she's a goner."

"And where does this leave you?" My patient mentor does not rush; he simply waits for my reply.

"Not sure. I was kind of into derby. But without that helmet, I don't stand a chance."

"Mizithra Achelois Moon, are you familiar with the tale of Dumbo?"

"Not particularly. I mean, it's something about a flying elephant. Is that the one you're talking about?"

Silas chuckles. He actually laughs. "Indeed. However, you may have missed a critical tenet of that parable. In the end, Dumbo discovers the magic feather given to him by the crows held no power at all. He possessed the ability to fly all along. It was always within."

The hairs on the back of my neck tingle. "Silas, are you saying what I think you're saying?"

"I am not the psychic. I would have no way of knowing what you surmise. Why don't you tell me what thoughts fill your mind?"

"I'm thinking you pulled a fast one on me, Silas Willoughby. It sounds like you're saying that helmet had no power. That somehow I can just skate."

"It is my understanding that athletic ability tends to run in families. Your grandmother was a fantastic derby skater, was she not?"

Oh brother! Another of his twisted phrases. Yes, she was not? No, she was not? "What are you getting at?"

He exhales a mixture of frustration tinged with a hint of sleepiness. "I must prepare some papers before they get to the sheriff's station. I'm sure you will come to understand this conundrum."

"Thanks for your help, Your *Sneakiness*."

He chuckles as he ends the call.

"So you can really skate? Is that what he was saying?" Erick's face looks like I feel — utterly overcome with disbelief.

My shoulders shrug of their own accord. "No idea. That man speaks in riddles. If he's saying that clumsy Mitzy Moon can somehow execute an apex jump with no otherworldly assistance . . . I have to see it to believe it."

Erick twists his hand back and forth on the steering wheel and chews the inside of his cheek. "So, are you gonna find a way to keep the derby team going?"

"I'm sure a wealthy heiress like myself can figure out something."

He reaches over, grips my hand, and squeezes it affectionately. "I know she can."

CHAPTER 23

THE ONLY TIME in my life I've felt this much anxiety in a hospital waiting room was after Erick had been shot. But that's another story.

The antiseptic odor and the bland, muted colors of the hospital only add to my unease. My fingernails are digging into my husband's hand, but he takes it like a champ.

The double doors from the operating room wing fly open, and the strained face of a doctor searches the smattering of waiting-room occupants.

"Csilla Galler?"

Luckily, Cellblock Dee shared Celia Fate's real name with me on the bus ride. I raise my hand like an overeager student in homeroom and try not to take offense when he gives my strange wardrobe a once over.

I couldn't access my abilities if I wanted to. Anxiety, worry, and a soupçon of fear have blocked everything.

"Are you the people who brought in Ms. Galler?"

Using his official voice, Erick fields the query. "That's correct. We are part of the law enforcement detachment dealing with the situation on Provincial 608."

The doctor's gaze falters, and he swallows as though his throat is constricted.

"Sorry to tell you, Ms. Galler's symptoms were irreversible."

My brain can't decipher the message. "Irreversible? Will she have some kind of permanent damage?"

"Ms. Galler presented with severe dehydration, hypothermia, and carbon monoxide poisoning." The doctor shifts his weight to the opposite foot and shakes his head. "The patient is deceased."

My knees turn to jelly. If not for the powerful arm of Erick Harper, I would be a puddle on the floor. I didn't know Celia Fate, but I know the absolute devastation of losing a parent. My mind is flooded with images of a faceless boy in Hungary who will never know how desperately his mother wished to return to him.

Erick nods and continues in a calm tone. "I'm

sure you did all you could, doctor. We'd like to see her. Say our goodbyes."

I'm not entirely sure what he has up his sleeve, but my brain swirls with too much fog to question his judgment.

The young doctor nods and leads us through the doors, down a series of hallways, and into an operating theater. He presses his lips together and gestures toward the cot. "Take as much time as you need. Speak with the nurse at the desk we passed when you've finished. I'm sorry for your loss."

He slips away without a sound.

Staring at the lifeless form on the gurney, my shoulders shake with silent sobs. Erick slips his arm around, pulls me close, and whispers, "We have to get her out of here. Her body could be tied up in an international incident for months. I'm sure some of the other women on the team know her family and will be able to help us return her home much more quickly."

Like a flash thunderstorm over a remote Pacific island, my sadness vanishes. I pull away and gaze into my husband's intense blue eyes. "Are you suggesting we steal a corpse?"

He shrugs and throws his hands in the air. "Honestly, I've got nothing. I just can't bear—"

"*Weekend at Bernie's!*" Without thinking, my inner film-school dropout latches onto this idea with everything I've got. We can get her back to her son. It's truly all that matters. Her loved ones need to say their final goodbye—

It's unclear how long I was catatonic, but the pace of Erick's fingers waving in front of my face and the concern in his voice means it's been more than a minute or two.

"I know that look, Moon. What exactly are you cooking up?"

A thick knot of emotion clogs my throat, and it takes several coughs to clear it. "At first, I was all in on the *Weekend at Bernie's* plan. We each scoop an arm around her and pretend like she's super drunk as we walk her out to your car."

He rolls his eyes. "I'm not sure the plot of some 80s movie is going to save us."

"Yeah. I agree. It was a long shot." Now might be a good time to mention that my happy place is film and television. Those lovely worlds that unfolded on the small screen saved me from oblivion during my years in foster care. Of course, the after-effect is that I tend to draw most of my real-world comparisons from that utterly fictional universe. *Comme ci comme ça.*

Erick shoves one hand into the pocket of his worn denim and tilts his head. "It feels like there's more."

"There is. I didn't tell you, because I was—"

He pulls me close. "Hey, no secrets. That's not just an agreement. That's a rule."

Drawing a ragged breath, I push on. "You're totally right. And I'll admit, I'm breaking the rule. Do you trust me?"

He inhales sharply, but replies, "Always."

"All right. Help me get her back into her derby clothes. I noticed an exit right before we made this last turn."

"I know you want this *Weekend at Bernie's* thing to work, Moon. If you'll trust *me*, I have a better idea."

Erick turns and rifles through the cabinets lining the far wall. He produces two sets of scrubs, head coverings, and masks. I throw the outfit on over my clothes, grab Celia's bag of personal items, and shove it under the blanket. My hand brushes against her cooling skin, and I shiver in fear.

Gotta shake it off. "We have to get her back to our place. Stat, doctor."

Walking toward the door of the surgical suite, I reach out with all my senses. "Coast is clear."

I open the door, and Erick pushes the gurney into the hallway. Then, we each take one side and walk with absolute confidence toward the first turn.

A nurse neither of us recognizes rounds the corner. Erick leans down as though he's listening to the patient, nods his head, and says. "We're taking you to the recovery room, ma'am."

The nurse offers a perfunctory smile and continues to wherever she's headed.

We hit the corner, look both ways, and make a beeline for the exit door.

"I'm counting on your sense of direction, Harper. I have no idea where we are."

He glances up at the sky, looks left and right, and proceeds with confidence.

Once the gurney is out of sight of the exit, he scoops up Celia, blanket and all, and breaks into a jog. I grab her bag of clothing and follow.

At the next corner, the parking lot is in view. The Nova sits about a hundred yards away in an emergency patient-only parking spot.

Erick reaches under his scrubs, into the pocket of his jeans, and tosses me a set of keys.

Shockingly, I catch them.

"Go open the trunk."

My big heart wants to protest, but trying to wedge a dead body into the back seat of a two-door muscle car would definitely take too long.

I find the key with the round top and run.

Once the trunk lid pops up, Erick is only a couple of strides behind me. He carefully places Celia in the trunk, I set her bag beside her, and in less than ten seconds, we're driving out of the lot.

Erick removes his hospital head covering and mask. I follow suit. He grabs his phone, and, even before I hear the beautiful French accent, I know beyond a shadow of a doubt he's calling CC.

"I need one last favor."

"I believe this is . . . how do you say . . . balance sheet? This ledger is in my favor now. You must promise that you and your gorgeous wife will come to Montréal — to my summer home. No excuses this time."

Erick looks at me. I nod emphatically.

"It's a deal. I'm going to need your help to get across the border. I have—"

"Do not tell me. Plausible deniability, my old friend."

"10-4."

We head down the main highway out of Crooks Bay, taking the fastest route to the border.

"Grab the wheel, Moon."

Having taken part in far too many car-related shenanigans in my misspent youth, I reach across without hesitation and steady the car while Erick rips off the top of his scrubs and returns to his civilian look.

His left hand grabs the wheel and his right squeezes my knee. "Take a deep breath. Do whatever you can, with whatever abilities you have, to appear as an absolutely calm and innocent tourist.

CC can pull strings, but only on his side of the border. We can assume these guys will all be on high alert after the roadblock, a busload of illegals, and who knows what else Paulsen told them?"

"Copy that."

The Nova is chewing up pavement as my mind wanders over every lesson my mentor has ever given me. I've perfected brief periods of invisibility, but only for myself. However, I can't come up with anything else that might save us. Especially if Paulsen is out there trying to cause trouble.

"Hey, hubby, I've got an idea. But I need you to pull over before we're in sight of the border. And give me a minute or two to get myself together."

He nods as though his wife simply told him she needed a quick cup of coffee and a doughnut.

We fly by a sign on the right that indicates the border is ten miles away.

Erick pulls off the road. "If I wait any longer, it's too risky. They have cameras on either side of the border to check for suspicious activity — pretty much just like this."

Blowing a raspberry, I attempt a hopeful tone. "Here's the thing, Harper. I think I can make us invisible. For maybe a minute or two. What can you do with that?"

He swallows hard, and his right hand twists on the steering wheel. "How sure are you?"

"About eighty percent."

"That will have to do. I'll get in close behind another vehicle. And when the gate goes up, I'll follow through. Sure hope you're right about this."

"You and me both, Harper."

There's a flurry of activity as the border gates pop into view. CC's red Mountie jacket stands out like a cherry on a vanilla sundae.

A big, dually truck pulls into the lane where the Canadian Mountie is chatting up a US border patrol agent.

Deep in my quiet inner space, I replay Mr. Willoughby's patient lesson.

His solid voice echoes in my mind. " You are not a solid object. You are a collection of atoms. Perhaps it would assist you to visualize a thread passing through the eye of a needle. A needle is a solid object made of steel. However, with care and patience, one is able to push a thread through the needle."

It was at this point in the lesson I reminded him that a needle has a hole in it. My doubt did not deter him.

He replied. "You have stumbled upon the trick. Remember that you are not solid. There is space between all the atoms that create the cells forming your body. You must allow the light to pass through these spaces. Only in this way will you succeed."

Here's hoping I can allow light to pass through — a bunch of stuff!

Erick tucks in tight behind the truck. The diesel fumes seep in and threaten to break my concentration. Can't risk it. Have to do this for Celia's little boy.

The truck in front of us passes a quick inspection and is waved through.

We follow so closely that I worry our bumper might get caught on the truck's tow hitch.

We pass through without issue, but I breathe my sigh of relief too soon.

I lose my focus — and our invisibility with it.

Lights and sirens blast into action, and Erick makes a dangerous evasive maneuver. He darts into the ditch beside the truck and rides in the giant shadow.

We're hitting speeds I don't want to think about, and then he switches off his headlights as we knife into darkness, illuminated by nothing more than a waning moon.

His phone rings, and I grab it.

An angry French-Canadian shouts over the line. "What are you doing? I was here! I had everything under control, my friend."

My breathing comes in gasps, and I reply as best I can. "It's a long story, CC. Erick can't talk right now. Anything you can do to misdirect the chase would be great. We can't wait to see Montréal."

Ending the call, the flashing lights behind us are getting further away by the second. Whether or not CC has anything to do with it, the lights soon vanish altogether.

Our high-speed chase simply becomes a high-speed race.

We fly by the city of Silver Shoals, and a smile hits me out of nowhere. "Hey, you can probably slow down, Speed Racer. We lost 'em."

The speedometer needle, which was buried, eases back a mere 10 mph.

"Didn't you promise to take me to some special bakery in Silver Shoals?"

My foolish question has the desired effect, and Erick laughs away the tension that had his shoulder blades knitted together. "You want me to turn around, Moon?"

"Not today. But maybe we can stop there on our way to Montréal?"

Another wave of laughter rolls off him. "Do you know how far it is to Montréal?" He shakes his head. "We'll be flying. But don't worry. I'll get you to Silver Shoals sooner or later."

We're making good time. Who wouldn't at these speeds?

The sign for Pin Cherry may as well be a lush oasis in the middle of the Sahara.

My heartbeat slows to almost normal, but then I remember the rest of my secret plan, and the poor thing nearly bangs out of my chest.

The real question is — do I have the courage?

CHAPTER 24

Erick pulls across First Avenue, parking facing the wrong way, directly in front of our steps.

He hands me the keys to the house, and he heads toward the trunk.

I unlock the front door while he scoops Celia into his arms and brings her inside.

"Put her on the couch."

He follows my instructions without question. Gotta love that man.

Approaching the fireplace, I begin counting bricks.

Two in . . . and . . . seven down. Pushing firmly, the brick pops out, revealing a secret compartment created by Silas Willoughby.

Erick turns and stares at me. Dumbfounded. "Has that always been there?"

"Silas." I throw my hands in the air. "I only found out about it this morning."

As I walk toward my husband, he glances at the object in my hand. "What's that?"

"It has a long name in a foreign language, and right now I'm too stressed to remember. But my mother called it the Oracle of Return."

"Your mother?" My husband scrunches up his face in disbelief.

"I don't have time to explain. It was a dream or something. I have to do this now before I lose my nerve."

"Lose your nerve? What are you talking about?" He steps between me and the sofa and crosses his arms.

Uh oh.

Despite my attempt to push off the conversation, it seems to be happening. I inhale sharply as tears roll down my cheeks. "My mother came to me in a visitation. Or, possibly, I went to her in some kind of out-of-body experience. Silas explained it better. Anyway, she told me about this statue. It's called the Oracle of Return. She told me if I whispered her name in its ear, she would return to me. Whole and unblemished."

Erick's breath escapes in a shocked exhale, and his arms fall to his sides. "You mean, alive? That statue in your hands can bring your mother back from the dead?"

"It can bring anyone back from the dead — once."

The full meaning of my words sink in, and Erick's gaze slowly travels to the prone figure on our sofa.

"You're going to use your one chance to bring your mother back to save this woman you don't even know?" His voice catches in his throat, and his eyes shine with emotion.

"I lost my mom a long time ago. I'll never stop missing her, but I've managed to create a happy life. I have a family, I have you, and I can talk to my mom — at least once in a while." Drawing a ragged breath, I continue. "There's a six-year-old boy back in Hungary who has no idea what happened to his mother. If I can spare him a lifetime of pain, I think it's worth it. Don't you?"

Erick throws his arms around me and kisses the top of my head. "You have to follow your heart, Mitzy. And I know how big your heart is." He steps back and wipes the tears from my cheek. "What do I need to do?"

With a weighty exhale, I lean into the planes of his chest. "Just give me a little room and maybe say a prayer for courage."

He loosens his hold on my shoulders and steps

back. His head bows. Whether or not he utters a prayer, I feel my chest swell with courage that comes from somewhere.

Kneeling beside Celia, I take a deep breath and attempt to focus. Holding the hunched stone statue in front of my face, I press my lips against its disproportionately large right ear and whisper, "Csilla Galler."

Energy hums in my hand. The stone shines bright blue, and suddenly transforms from a dingy ancient object to a glowing sphere of atoms. A brilliant flash takes my breath away, and what was once a statue is now a swirl of glowing dust that enters Celia's nostrils.

The room falls silent.

Nothing happens.

Shakily, I climb to my feet and turn toward Erick. "Maybe I did something wrong. Maybe I wasted—" Sobs wrack my body.

He slips his arm around me. "Should we call Silas?"

Nodding my head, I reach for my phone.

Swiping away my tears, I attempt to focus on the screen.

Erick's awestruck voice shatters the quiet. "Look!"

A subtle glow emanates from Celia's body, beginning at her head and inching its way down to her toes.

As the glow fades, she gasps for air.

My phone clatters to the floor, and I fall to my knees beside her. "Celia? You're safe. Atlas has been—"

Huge green eyes gaze at me in wonder. She appears to be struggling to see clearly.

"You're safe." I don't know what else to say.

Finally, she lifts her wobbly hand and points. "Here? Where is this?"

"You're in Pin Cherry Harbor. My husband, Erick, saved you from the bus. Atlas Hahn has been arrested. We're going to get you home. You're going to see your son."

Her hands shoot up and grip my shoulders with surprising force.

"My boy? I will see my boy?"

"We're going to get you back to Hungary as soon as you are well enough to travel."

Her fingers dig into my arms. "Now. Please. I travel now."

I'm unfamiliar with the subtleties of powerful relics, but I'm very familiar with a mother's love. If she believes she's well enough to travel, who am I to question?

Glancing at Erick, I shrug. "Can you book a

ticket? Her passport is likely in the box I told Boomer about on the bus."

"10-4." He kneels beside me and whispers for my ears only. "You're sure she wasn't the one driving the van?"

Maybe the Oracle of Return gave Celia some superhuman hearing, because she immediately sits up and addresses Erick directly. "I don't drive. No shifting. I do not shifting."

Glancing at Erick, a realization washes over me. "Celia couldn't have been driving. You said yourself the van you found was a four-speed. When he got on the bus, Atlas announced he was the only one who could drive a stick shift. There's absolutely no way Celia was behind the wheel."

Erick breathes a tremendous sigh of relief. "Good enough for me. I'll book tickets right now. Can you give her something to wear?"

"I'm pretty sure I've got plenty to spare." Soft laughter breaks the tense moment.

Erick heads to the computer, and I explain to Celia that she needs some clothing for her trip. As I lead her toward the exit into the bookshop, I call over my shoulder, "Remember to get her passport from Boomer."

"10-4."

When Celia and I enter the bookshop, she stops

and gazes around the dim interior in awe. "This is yours?"

"Yes, my grandmother left this all to me when she — in her will." There. I didn't even have to stretch the truth. As we circle up the stairs to the Rare Books Loft, I send a psychic message to Grams.

I'm bringing a guest into the closet. She needs clothing and nothing more. Please don't scare her.

No response.

The secret bookcase door slides open. Celia gasps and presses her hand to her chest.

"My grandmother loved secret rooms."

The recently resurrected woman nods, but her mouth remains open.

When we enter my old apartment, Grams spins away from the computer, displaying an expression laden with guilt.

Announcing to no one in particular, I restate my mission. "We are simply here to get Celia some clothes before she gets on her flight back to Hungary. Nothing more."

Grams pantomimes zipping her lips together, locking them, and tucking the invisible key in her cleavage. Fortunately, I manage to avoid laughing.

Pyewacket lifts his head from the four-poster bed, stretches twice, and approaches Celia. She leans against me. "Is wild?"

"He lives here. Pyewacket can be dangerous, but something about his expression tells me he likes you. It's all right."

She crouches, and Pyewacket moves close enough to allow Celia to scratch his broad tan head. She smiles and gazes at me. "My boy, he love the cat."

"I'm sure your son is going to love everything in life a little more once you get home."

Guiding her into the closet, I ignore her shocked expression and rifle through the drawers to find her a reasonable outfit for her trip.

Her feet are a little smaller than mine, so I offer her two pairs of socks to take up the gap in the shoes.

Other than that, we have her dressed and ready for her flight in no time.

She asks to use the bathroom, and while she's in the restroom, I grab a handful of cash from another drawer in my closet.

When she returns, I hand her a coat and push the cash into the pocket. "You'll need this for your trip. I'm so sorry about what happened with Atlas Hahn. I promise you he will pay for everything he did." My snoopy nature needs closure. "Celia, why did Atlas tie you up?"

Emotion twists her features, and she draws a

ragged breath. "I see things. He kills this boy, and—"

"You were in the van?"

She nods and presses her fingers to her mouth.

"I don't want you to get detained at the police station, but we need your statement. Can I record a video of you? Can you tell me exactly what happened?"

Celia glances around nervously. "Is okay. Yes."

Pulling out my phone, I encourage her to start from the beginning.

She fell asleep in the backseat of the van. When they got back to the house where all the women live, the derby gals just let her sleep.

The next thing she remembers is waking to a large crash. "I scream. Atlas backs away. The boy . . . he bleeds. Atlas say to keep mouth shut." Sobs consume her.

Thoughts of her young son must be breaking her heart.

"Did you tell anyone?"

She nods once. "I try to steal a phone. This poor boy. His mother . . . Atlas has only phone. He sleeps. I sneak in. I press 9-1-1." A sob chokes off her words.

"He woke up, didn't he?"

She covers her face with both hands and cries.

Grabbing a box of tissues, I pause the video and

let her pull herself together. "I need you to finish the story — for the sheriff."

"Okay. I do this." Celia tells of Atlas binding and gagging her and locking her in a closet. He transferred her into the bus the night before our big bout.

That cruel man must've taken her over there right after I texted him.

Celia fills in the last few details, and, when she heads into the part of the story concerning her rescue, I stop the video. No sense creating any record of how Erick and I got her across the border and brought her back to life!

She looks at the phone and then toward me. Oceans of hope surge from her. "I go home now?"

The bookcase slides open, and Erick walks in holding three pieces of paper and a passport. "I ran over to the station, and Deputy Johnson let me *inspect* this passport. Boomer ran interference for me."

"Nice job, Harper. I've got her statement on video, so we've got all our bases covered." Turning to Celia, I rub her shoulder. "You can go home."

Erick nods. "There's a Piper tri-pacer waiting at the airport. She's got a connection in Chicago, and she'll be in Hungary tomorrow. Did you give her money?"

"Absolutely. Seems like we're all set?"

He smiles. "All set. I can take her to the airport."

Celia cringes.

"I think I better take her. You understand."

"I absolutely understand." Erick tosses me the keys to the Nova.

They land on the floor at my feet. We all knew that was happening. Even psychic luck runs out at some point.

Celia and I drive to the airport in silence, and I wait until I see the tiny fixed-wing aircraft leave the runway before I head back to the car.

Sitting in the airport parking lot, I clasp my precious dreamcatcher necklace, which once hung around my mother's neck, and whisper, "Mama, I hope you forgive me. I hope you understand — I had to."

I hold my breath and hope to hear her voice.

Nothing.

Then the nearest streetlight blinks off and back on with unnatural brightness.

A flush of warmth spreads through my chest.

"Thank you, Mama. I love you too."

CHAPTER 25

MORNING BRINGS A FLURRY OF ACTIVITY! Silas is working miracles with Immigration and Naturalization Service, while Boomer ensures Atlas Hahn pays for every single one of his crimes, including money laundering.

That last one is thanks to the hot gossip from Tally about the deposits they were making at the bank.

They even throw kidnapping onto the list after I share the video of Csilla "Celia Fate" Galler's statement.

Erick and I are pondering the options with the roller derby team, over enormous sticky caramel rolls and steaming mugs of coffee at the diner.

"It's not a question of money, hubby. We can afford to do whatever we need to keep it going. But at last count, eight of the women had chosen to return to Hungary and Croatia. The six who want to stay need housing, jobs, and will have to go through the legal immigration process."

Erick pulls a hunk of caramel roll off the main piece, shoves it in, and licks the frosting from his fingers.

Dear Lord, baby Jesus! How's a girl supposed to concentrate?

He glances across the table and chuckles. "Did you lose your train of thought?"

"Hilarious, Harper. What are we gonna do?"

"Why don't you buy the laundromat?"

"What will that do?"

"I'm sure Hahn was cooking the books, but I honestly think Pin Cherry needs a laundromat. You could set up the women who want to stay local in the living quarters above that place, at least temporarily. Plus, two or three of them could work there."

"What about Tammy?"

"Who?"

I drop my head and exhale with frustration. "Tammy Samson. She quit her other two jobs because she was making more money as a night manager, remember?" He nods. "So if I buy it and put the derby gals in charge, how will she pay for her daughter's care facility?"

Erick takes a long sip of coffee and wipes the corners of his mouth with the thin paper napkin. "That family has been through it, Moon. Maybe your philanthropic foundation could pay for the daughter's care? Take that burden off their plate, you know?"

Before responding, I actually finish chewing and swallowing a bite of food. "I like where your head's at. What about the rest of their bills? Groceries, utilities, you know — day-to-day stuff?"

"I'll pay Ken a visit. His addled brain still thinks I'm the sheriff. So—"

"And you will be again." I wink and flash my eyebrows.

He sighs and bows with humility. "Anyway, I'll make sure Tammy gets every one of those disability checks. And, using your grandmother's inspiration, I'll set Ken up in the program. I know a couple people who head up the local AA chapter. Maybe something good can come out of this mess."

"I wish Jason Samson hadn't turned to selling drugs. I guess he was desperate, but hustling pool or—"

"Easy, Miss Delinquent. I hate to see anyone leave this earth too soon. The trouble is, Jason made those choices. Maybe he was concerned about his family at first, but what Boomer has uncovered about that campus drug operation is shocking. That kid was pulling down big money. Greed took over, and, well, you know what happened."

We quietly finish our caramel rolls, and Tally slips by, refills our mugs, and moves on. She didn't become the best waitress in Birch County by accident. Tally can read a room better than most psychics.

My grandfather steps up to the table and leans over the piece of paper sitting between Erick and me. "You gonna need a coach for the team?"

"Yeah. I've been trying to talk Erick into it, but you know his plans."

Odell feigns innocence for a moment, but breaks into a smile and nods. "Everyone in town knows your husband's plans."

Picking up my mug of coffee, I lean back against the red vinyl. "You have someone in mind?"

He sniffs sharply and scrapes a hand through his grey buzz cut. "I know quite a bit about the game. Coaches don't have to skate, as long as they know how it's supposed to be done."

And I thought I was the queen of stuff coming out of left field. "Are you serious? When would you find the time?"

"Well, I been meaning to talk to you about that." He bobs his head at me, and I budge over to make room. Odell slides into the booth and places his arm around my shoulders. "Tally is going to take over."

Pulling away, I nearly spill my coffee. Gramps puts a steadying hand on my mug and acts like I'm a toddler having a tantrum. "Settle down, kid. At the speed of this changeover, it'll be ten years before I'm fully out of the kitchen. But Tally made me a great offer, and I'm carrying the note for her. We'll be training up a new cook, so I'm gonna have some free time. Something I haven't had in about fifty years."

My throat tightens, and there's an ache in my chest. Silas talking about time marching on, and now Odell announcing his retirement. Things are changing in Pin Cherry Harbor, and I'm not sure if I like it.

"No one is going to be able to make my scrambled eggs and chorizo the way you do, Gramps. And who's gonna remember to order that one bottle of Tabasco every six months?"

He glances over at Erick, and they share a knowing smile. Odell leans toward me, kisses the top of my head, and slides out of the booth. "I'd never leave you hanging, kid. If the new cook doesn't meet with your approval, he or she will be out on their ear." He raps his knuckles twice on the silver-flecked white Formica and returns to the kitchen.

Erick walks his fingers across the table and turns his palm up. I shove both of my hands into his as I blink back tears. "Everything's changing. My Pin Cherry is turning into something else."

A one-sided smirk lifts the corner of his pouty mouth and his eyes sparkle with mischief. "Now you know how I felt the day you wandered into town, tripped, and fell on me."

Yanking my hands back to my side of the table, my lips part to launch into my standard defense. Before I can get two words out, Erick slides onto my bench seat and his soft lips brush my cheek. "You'll have your hands full running the investigations office. I submitted your paperwork this morning."

"It's official? I'm private investigator Mitzy Moon?"

He chuckles. "For all intents and purposes, yes. We'll get something official in the mail in a week or two, but you met all the requirements. Plus, you've got the best 'solve' record in the county, probably in all of almost-Canada."

I snake my arms around his neck and kiss him fiercely. "I never could've done it without you, Harper the Hero."

CUT TO—

My first bout as team captain. Odell is still getting the hang of coaching, but, after plastering the community college with posters and recruiting enough fresh meat to fill the roster, the Pin Cherry Rink Rashers are back on top.

It was difficult to say goodbye to the gals who chose to go home, but I supported their decision one hundred percent.

Bam Wow, Betty Beware, Cellblock Dee, Barb Erica, Mona Madness, and Silence of the Jams all stayed. They're flourishing, and three of them have enrolled at the community college where we're now skating.

These younger girls on the team have so much energy; makes me feel like an old lady. Creeping up on thirty, I'm not sure how I feel about that. Grams tells me I don't know the first thing about getting old! She's probably right. My life experience is admittedly limited.

I hear travel expands the mind.

Erick and I leave for our belated honeymoon trip to Europe next month. I'm extremely excited to start our journey in Budapest, Hungary.

Our first stop will be meeting Csilla Galler's son, then we'll get together with the rest of the gals, before we take a little cruise on the Danube.

I'm hoping we're able to take in as many sites as we can cram into a three-week trip.

My hubby still has no idea, mind you. When he

said no secrets, I conveniently decided that surprises don't fit into that category. He should know by now that if there's a loophole to be found, Mitzy Moon will find it.

End of Book 6

But, the mysteries continue...
Curl up with the next book in the Harper and
Moon Investigations series!

A NOTE FROM TRIXIE

Oh, my goodness! I love roller derby! Thank you for joining Mitzy and Erick on their new adventures in **Harper and Moon Investigations**. As always, I'll keep writing them if you keep reading . . .

The best part of "living" in Pin Cherry Harbor continues to be feedback from my early readers. Thank you to my alpha readers/cheerleaders, Angel, Scott, and Erin. HUGE thanks to my fantastic beta readers who always give me actionable and honest feedback: Veronica McIntyre and Nadine Peterse-Vrijhof. And big "small town" hugs to the world's best ARC Team – Trixie's Mystery ARC Detectives!

My patient editor Philip Newey provided important notes on a couple of plot holes. Many thanks to him! I enjoy getting his feedback as I improve each case. I'd also like to give a shout out to Roxx at Proof Perfect for the spot-on proofing! Any remaining errors are my own.

Big thanks to Lisa for setting up the important tour of the "bus barn" with Vicki. I learned some wonderful stuff!

FUN FACT: I played roller derby for two years and we sponsored a team this year!

My favorite line from this case: "No one in this town can keep a secret. The whole place would grind to a halt if the gossip stopped flowing." ~Mitzy

I'm currently writing book seven in the **Harper and Moon Investigations** series, *Scripts and Empty Crypts.* All your *Mitzy Moon Mysteries* series favorites will continue on — but there will definitely be a murder!

Thank you for continuing to hang out with us.

Trixie Silvertale (February 2025)

SCRIPTS AND EMPTY CRYPTS

Harper and Moon Investigations No. 7

When a movie production turns into murder, will our psychic sleuth find the killer on the call sheet?

Mitzy Moon has gotten too comfortable. She's happily put down roots in Pin Cherry Harbor and feels safe. If only she'd paid closer attention to the whisperings of her not-as-dearly-departed-as-everyone-thinks grandmother...

Without warning, Mitzy and her fiendish feline

are thrown into the middle of a television series about their life! Grams sold the rights, and the production has descended on the bookshop. The inept crew disturbed the wrong crypt, and now a vengeful spirit may be loose.

Can Mitzy flip the script on this murderer, or will this be her final scene?

Scripts and Empty Crypts is the seventh book in the hilarious paranormal cozy mystery series, Harper and Moon Investigations, a spinoff from the popular Mitzy Moon Mysteries. If you like snarky heroines, supernatural intrigue, and a dash of romance, then you'll love Trixie Silvertale's rollicking page-turner.

Buy Scripts and Empty Crypts to roll credits on a killer today!

Grab yours!
https://readerlinks.com/l/5211933

Scan this QR Code with the camera on your phone. You'll be taken right to the next Harper and Moon Investigations case.

Once you're in the Club, you'll also be the first to receive

updates from Pin Cherry Harbor and access to giveaways, new release announcements, short stories, behind-the-scenes secrets, and much more!

Scan this QR Code with the camera on your phone. You'll be taken right to the page to join the Club and get your FREE Novella!

THANK YOU!

Trying out a new book is always a risk and I'm thankful that you rolled the dice with Mitzy Moon. If you loved the book, the sweetest thing you can do (*even sweeter than pin cherry pie à la mode*) is to leave a review so that other readers will take a chance on Mitzy, Erick, and the gang.

Don't feel you have to write a book report. A brief comment like, "Can't wait to read the next book in this series!" will potential readers make their choice.

Leave a quick review HERE
ttps://readerlinks.com/l/4407364

Thank you, and I'll see you in Pin Cherry Harbor!

Mitzy Moon Mysteries

Heists and Poltergeists: Paranormal Cozy Mystery

Blades and Bridesmaids: Paranormal Cozy Mystery

Scones and Tombstones: Paranormal Cozy Mystery

Vandals and Yule Scandals: Paranormal Cozy Mystery

Harper and Moon Investigations

Ropes and Last Hopes: Paranormal Cozy Mystery

Bells and Bombshells: Paranormal Cozy Mystery

Rodeo Clowns and Shakedowns: Paranormal Cozy Mystery

Stiffs and Petroglyphs: Paranormal Cozy Mystery

Fatal Wines and Valentines: Paranormal Cozy Mystery

April Curses and May Hearses: Paranormal Cozy Mystery

Wheels and Dirty Deals: Paranormal Cozy Mystery

Scripts and Empty Crypts: Paranormal Cozy Mystery

Christmas Catastrophe Mysteries

Peppermint Cookie Murder: Paranormal Cozy Mystery

Apple Dumpling Murder: Paranormal Cozy Mystery

Linzer Cookie Murder: Paranormal Cozy Mystery

Chocolate Crinkle Cookie Murder: Paranormal Cozy Mystery

...more to come!

MAGICAL RENAISSANCE FAIRE MYSTERIES

Explore the world of Coriander the Conjurer. A fortune-telling fairy with a heart of gold!

Book 1:

All Swell That Ends Spell – A dubious festival. A fatal swim. Can this fortune-telling fairy herald the true killer?

Book 2:

Fairy Wives of Windsor – A jolly Faire. A shocking murder. Can this furtive fairy outsmart the killer?

Book 3:

Double Double Royal Trouble – When a treat-peddling witch is found dead, will this cursed faire crumble?

Join Sydney Coleman and her unruly ghosts, as they solve mysteries in a truly haunted mansion!

Book 1: ***Moonlight and Mischief*** – She's desperate for a fresh start, but is a mansion on sale too good to be true?

Book 2: ***Moonlight and Magic*** – A haunted Halloween tour seem like the perfect plan, until there's murder...

Book 3: ***Moonlight and Mayhem*** – An unwelcome
visitor. A surprising past. Will her fire sale end in smoke?

ABOUT THE AUTHOR

USA TODAY Bestselling author Trixie Silvertale grew up reading an endless supply of Lilian Jackson Braun, Hardy Boys, and Nancy Drew novels. She loves the amateur sleuths in cozy mysteries and obsesses about all things paranormal. Those two passions unite in her Harper and Moon Investigations, and she's thrilled to write them and share them with you.

When she's not consumed by writing, she bakes to fuel her creative engine and pulls weeds in her herb garden to clear her head (*and sometimes she pulls out her hair, but mostly weeds*).

Greetings are welcome:
trixie@trixiesilvertale.com

BB bookbub.com/authors/trixie-silvertale

f facebook.com/TrixieSilvertale

O instagram.com/trixiesilvertale

www.ingramcontent.com/pod-product-compliance
Lightning Source LLC
Chambersburg PA
CBHW030125180626
46812CB00002B/560